SADISTIC
LEATHERCOPS

First Edition

Published by
The Nazca Plains Corporation
Las Vegas, Nevada
2011

ISBN: 978-1-61098-178-1
E-book: 978-1-61098-179-8

Published by

The Nazca Plains Corporation ®
4640 Paradise Rd, Suite 141
Las Vegas NV 89109-8000

PUBLISHER'S NOTE
Sadistic Leathercops is a work of fiction created wholly by G.W. Leatherman PARKS' imagination. All characters are fictional and any resemblance to any persons living or deceased is purely by accident. No portion of this book reflects any real person or events.

Cover, Fleshblack
Art Director, Blake Stephens

DEDICATION

TO: My Leatherbuddy Jim Maciel, Founder and Guiding Spirit of FITS LIKE A GLOVE (F.L.A.G.), who gave me the opportunity to present my Leather stories to a wider audience; and, TO: J.C.R., My favorite Leatherboy.

SADISTIC
LEATHERCOPS

First Edition

G.W. Leatherman PARKS

CONTENTS

CHAPTER 1

Sadistic Cops

The men walked down the darkened, litter-strewn alley. It was a dangerous place to be, but both were willing to take the risk.

The men's heavy engineer boots resounded against the concrete paving. The men ignored the graffiti spray painted on the brick walls of the buildings. At one point, a pathetic pile of clothing turned out to be a human being, strung out on drugs. He asked for money. The two men snorted and continued their journey.

"Tito has to be around here somewhere... I know he deals in this fucking alley. Where the fuck is he?" said the taller of the two men. Both men were in black Leather motorcycle jackets and chaps. They also wore black Leather executioner's hoods to protect their anonymity.

"Relax, if he wants to make a deal... he'll find us." responded the other man.

"Man, I need some of Tito's weed. He always has the best fucking weed in town. This fucking week would have put anyone else in the hospital."

"Well, then, you came to the right place..." a voice seemingly materialized from a darkened doorway.

"Tito, how the fuck you doing?" said the taller of the Leatherclad men.

The Latino, heavily-muscled, emerged from the doorway. His hand was firmly gripping a plastic bag of weed. His forearms covered in religious tattoos were flexed just in case the two clients tried to cause any trouble. A sharpened stiletto resided in his pants pocket.

"My price has gone up... this is premium weed... $150."

"What the fuck, Tito? You crazy?"

Tito's hand slid into his pocket, his fingers wrapping around the handle of the stiletto knife.

"Take it or leave it, fucker," Tito countered. His brown eyes burned with defiance. His pecs flexed underneath his sleeveless tee shirt.

The two Leathermen advanced toward Tito, their gloved fists doubled up. Tito whipped out his knife and began making slashing advances toward the two men. Even though he was muscled, he was no match for the two beefy men. One soon had him in a chokehold and the other pocketed the stash of marijuana. The taller of the two gutpunched Tito twice, just to let him know who was boss. Tito knew he was in trouble, he instinctively knew the two were cops, but had been selling to them for about two months. They never questioned his price, always paid in cash. But there was something about them – they were too clean-cut – no facial hair, regulation haircuts. 'Fuck,' he thought. "I can't get locked up again," Tito thought as a black bandana was tied tightly around his eyes. Tito was lifted by the two beefy men and carried a distance. He was thrown into the trunk of a car. The two Leathermen stripped off their Leather jackets and chaps, revealing the blue uniforms of the city's police force.

The cops went back to the headquarters where they reported the activities of the day to their captain. Well, for the most part.

"We got a lead on a street-level dealer who has connections with the higher ups...," Morris explained, "street name is Tito. We were in the neighborhood he sells in, and we cruised the alleys where he sets up shop, but, ah... we didn't find him, boss." Both men looked at the wall above their captain's head, avoiding eye contact. "Okay," the captain advised, "keep on that beat for another day or two. Sooner or later someone will rat him out." The two men clocked out and retreated to the patrol car. As Morris rounded the car to get into the driver's seat, he thumped the trunk.

"Fuck, yeah, Hank," he boasted as he turned on the ignition, "We got some pussy and some weed for tonight."

The two spent a lot of time together as patrol cops. Their patrolling had spilled over to their private time. And as Leathermen who shared the pleasures of S&M. They especially enjoyed working over bad boys, like Tito who currently resided in the trunk of the patrol car.

The two men peeled out of the parking lot with their captive in the trunk. As they drove toward Morris' house, they outlined the plan for Tito's abuse. Morris lived a good thirty minutes away from HQ, far from inquiring minds. His house was a comfortable rancher equipped with a basement dungeon. Although Hank maintained an apartment near HQ, the men spent most of their time at Morris' house, fucking each other or working over a captive boy.

"Damn, let me at those tits," Morris said as he lit a cigarette, "I can't wait to roll those nips between my fingers."

Extracting a cigarette from the same pack, Hank remarked, "Fuck, yeah, I grabbed his ass. He's got a meaty ass just ready to be plowed."

"Did you get a look at his equipment?" Morris pondered.

"He was squirming too much for me to feel his rod, but I'll bet that boy's hung."

The men pulled into Morris' garage. Extracting Tito from the trunk was challenging – he was not going willingly, but the two beefy cops eventually succeeded in wrestling him down the steps and onto a workover table.

Four heavy Leather restraints held Tito's wrists and ankles in place. An additional Leather belt was strapped across Tito's heaving chest after Morris had cut away Tito's tee shirt.

"Look at those fucking nips, man!" Morris exclaimed as he grabbed a handful of titflesh in each hand.

The two men quickly hooded their faces before removing the black bandana, not giving Tito a chance to see their faces.

With more difficulty, Hank removed the black bandana and quickly hooded the boy with a black Leather hood, which laced in the back and allowed the boy breathing ability through nostril holes. A strapped on plug was inserted in the mouth hole so the boy wouldn't verbalize during the impending session.

Morris retrieved the cycle jackets and chaps from the patrol car before the men went upstairs to shed their uniforms. They took their time, hoping the boy would settle down while they changed into full Leather.

Both men were beefy and they admired each other in the mirror above the bureau. They worked out side by side in a nearby gym at least three times a week and it showed.

Hank playfully grabbed Morris' ass, "Damn, I'd like to rape you right here, right now."

They wrestled, landing on the bed. Feeling each other's naked flesh. Cock pressed against cock. Nips against nips. Tongues exploring each other's mouths.

After a time, however, their mutual horny thoughts returned to the new conquest in the dungeon.

The men outfitted themselves in the black Leathers worn during the capture. Their meaty manrods sequestered in studded codpieces attached to Leather jockstraps. The hoods were put back on. Clipping cigars, they returned downstairs.

It was obvious that the prisoner was not happy in his new surroundings. He was pulling on all four restraints, leaving reddened marks on his wrists. His military boots protected his ankles from a similar assault. His head was jerking from side to side and he was swearing at them in Spanish.

The men chuckled as they lighted their cigars and watched in continued amusement.

"You'll settle down, boy." Morris shouted, as he leaned over the hooded face of Tito, "there's no escape, fucker."

Hank walked over to the dungeon wall and retrieved a braided flogger and a pair of titclamps from the extensive collection of torture devices.

He handed the clamps to Morris with a grin on his face. "I know what you want to concentrate on." Morris began by kneading the titflesh of the boy with his gloved hands. He rolled the nips between his thumb and finger until the nips were erect.

"Fuck, look at those, bro. They are handsome." With that, he took the lighted end of the cigar and ran it around the boy's tits. A healthy (but stifled) scream came from the boy. Morris' cock hardened in its codpiece as he continued to encircle the nips with the burning cigar. "Fuck, yeah," Morris crowed, "I've got his attention."

Hank began flogging the boy's chest, each time approaching the boy's privates one stroke closer. The boy's faded blue jeans still protected his cock and balls.

Hank stopped the flogging momentarily to reveal the boy's manhood. He was not disappointed. A handsome cock and balls in a very loose ballsac were revealed.

Hank began playing with Tito's cock – it was getting aroused by the touch of the Leather on the naked skin. The balls hung down to the table.

With the cockshaft held firmly in his gloved hand, Hank began slapping the boy's dick. The boy was moaning, cursing, rocking his head from side to side. With the cock fully aroused, Hank wrapped bondage rope around it. He then pulled on the ballsac until he had successfully wrapped the bondage rope around each extension of the sac, separating the nuts. The remainder of the rope was secured to a hook above the boy's head. With one hand, Hank worked the cock and balls while he flogged the boy's ribcage with the other. Reddened marks appeared.

"We're making progress here, bro." Morris remarked as he laughed at the bound boy, "Let's take out the plug."

He reached up and pulled the plug out of the boy's mouth.

"You fucking assholes. Let me out of here. I'll kill you. I will shove your balls down your throat... My brothers will seek you out and work you over...."

"Fuck you, bitch. You ain't gonna do jackshit." With that, Morris leaned over and spit tobacco juice in the captive's mouth. The boy sputtered as Morris clamped the plug back in place. Morris let loose with a series of slaps to the cheeks of the captive. He went back to molesting the boy's titflesh, finally placing the clamps on the boy's nips. The alligator teeth bit into the titflesh as the boy emitted yet another scream.

The two Leathermen worked side-by-side, increasing the pressure on the clamps, and increasing the pressure on the balls and cock by tightening the lead to the hook in the ceiling.

"Let's leave the boy to simmer for a while, handsome," Morris said to Hank. Hank was in agreement as the two cops went back upstairs.

They settled in front of the television to watch basketball. They planned the next session as they absently watched the basketball game. Hank pulled the confiscated weed from his Leather jacket pocket and rolled a joint for himself and one for Morris.

They drew deeply on the joints.

"Tito was right – this is good shit. Worth every penny we paid for it," said Morris as both of them laughed.

As the game ended, the two cops were anxious to continue the assault on the prisoner.

They found the prisoner moaning, his head rocking from side to side.

"Time to flip him over, bro."

With difficulty, they did. Tito was more willing to cooperate because his balls and cock were still attached to the lead suspended from the ceiling. As he was laid on his belly, his cock and balls had to be maneuvered so that they were positioned between his asscheeks.

"Damn, Hank, look at that fucking ass! I want to work that over..." With that, Morris gave a healthy slap to the left asscheek. With a grin on his face, he couldn't resist and let loose with a few more. Even though Tito's ass was initially clenched tight, it would not remain so for long. Both Hank and Morris had other plans. Morris pulled a Leather butt paddle off the wall while Hank retrieved an inflatable dildo.

Morris began paddling. And when Morris paddled a boy's ass he couldn't stop. He enjoyed the sound the paddle made as it struck the flesh of a boy's ass. He delivered blow after blow. His cock was throbbing in its cod. Hank was content, for the moment, to work on Tito's cock and balls. The cock was throbbing and the balls were tight. He slathered them with lube, working Tito's cock into a frenzy as Morris continued to paddle the boy's ass unmercifully. Tito's ass was reddened with several white welts appearing.

The appearance of the welts did not slow down Hank or Morris. It fueled them in their sadistic tendencies. They began a more intense flogging of Tito's back. Tito began a keening sound as each lash struck his back.

"Take it like the tough punk you are!" Hank growled.

"Ain't talking tough now, are you, boy?"

As each flogged, the two Leathermen fondled their crotches. Both cocks were pulsating within their Leather pouches as the men rotated the floggers they were using. Braided Leather, latigo strips, tails of different Leathers, paddles, single tail. The boy's back was crisscrossed with welts. In several places, the welts had broken open and beads of blood were evident. The shoulders, shoulder blades, upper arms, back, ribcage and asscheeks were all marked with the Leathermen's flogmarks.

It was time to tackle the boy's ass, which both the men approached with a special pleasure. The boy's cock and balls were released from their rope bondage as Hank crawled on top of the victim. Hank's fist was the first to explore the boy's tight hole. But Morris' fist wasn't far behind. By this time, Tito was screaming continuously. The screaming fell on deaf ears. These men were only interested in their own pleasures. Tito was just the vessel for their sadism.

Morris' fist was like a corkscrew in a wine bottle, inching its way up the boy's rectum. Tito had apparently never been fisted and was pulling on his restraints.

Hank finally held the boy's head down on the table. "This will go a lot easier for you if you just relax, boy." Tito's muffled protests just incited the cops to continue their interrogation.

The boy shook his head as much as he could. Hank's iron grip immobilized it very effectively, however.

The fist worked its way into Tito's ass. As Morris crawled on to the table, his swollen cock replaced his fist. Morris had a look of contentment on his face as his cock glided in and out of the boy's virgin fuckhole. Morris had a big cock and to find a hole this receptive was reward enough for capturing Tito.

Hank was rubbing his swollen cock. He unsnapped his cod and his cock sprang forth. He retrieved a spreader from the shelf of toys and popped it in Tito's mouth. There was now no possibility that Tito's teeth could bite down on his manrod. He pulled Tito's jaw upward and thrust his big cock into Tito's mouth. Like it or not, Tito now had a man's hardened fuckpole in his mouth.

"This is my nightstick, boy," Hank taunted as he thrust the cock further and further into the boy's mouth.

Both men were thoroughly enjoying the session. They wanted to prolong it as long as possible. While manipulating his cock in and out of Tito's mouth, Hank pulled a small plastic bag out of his jacket pocket with two more joints. He lighted them and handed one to Morris.

As they continued to pump their cocks in Tito's unwilling holes, they drew heavily on the weed supplied by their fuckboy.

With their horniness accelerating with the weed, the two men began a more frantic pumping. One large cock up Tito's unwilling ass, one in his unwilling mouth.

Morris' body slammed forward as he shot a load up the boy's ass. Hank kept pumping aware that his partner had lubricated the boy's ass with his seed. He wanted to spread his seed down the boy's throat. He soon did just that.

While Tito heaved and then remained silent, the two Leathermen gripped each other and soon were engaged in deep-throat kissing. Their Leathered bodies connecting, muscled arms pulling each other closer to one another. Morris' cum-covered cock rubbed against Hank's throbbing rod — combining their seed, making both cocks instantly erect once again. Morris reached down and rubbed the shafts of their two cocks. Hank clutched Morris' ass. The men enjoyed the taste of each other's mouths. Both men began to sweat, their nips rubbing against one another's. Sweat pouring from underneath their hooded faces down their chests and down their back. Each reaching around and fingering their partner's ass. Cock pressed against cock. Balls slapping against one another's.

The intense manfuck session continued for some time until the men could hold their sperm no longer. Cords of cum shot out of each cock, combining and slathering the men's Leathered legs. The tongues continued to explore. Licking the sweat off of each other's body. Squeezing asscheeks. Pulling on tits. Massaging each other's muscular backs and arms.

Hank finally pulled away, "Damn! That felt so fucking good. But, Mo, what do we do about him?" as he pointed toward their captive.

"We have a long talk with him."

They released the prisoner from the workover table but led him to a St. Andrew's Cross. He did not put up much of a struggle, apparently exhausted from the workover. They restrained him face forward.

Tito's head lolled to one side. His ass was sore from the invasion. His mouth was still spread wide open.

"All right, listen up, boy." Tito did not respond for which he was slapped hard across the face.

"I SAID LISTEN TO ME, BOY!" as Hank slapped him hard across the face once again. That seemed to get Tito's attention.

"You will not say anything to anybody about this… or your ass will be in jail and you will be some handsome prisoner's fuckboy. We'll put the word out that you like cock up your ass and down your throat. And you'll be gang raped… Understood, boy?"

The boy slowly shook his head signifying his compliance.

The two cops, still in Leather and hoods, redressed the boy. His knife was confiscated. He was blindfolded, restrained, and put in the back seat of the patrol car. They drove Tito to his neighborhood and dumped him in an alley. He crawled to a doorway and remained there for the night.

CHAPTER 2

Two Punks

The alarm went off at 5:30am. It roused both the men from sound sleep.

Both slowly got out of bed, rubbing their tumescent cocks. They both made their way to the bathroom where Morris turned on the hot water for the shower.

The two crawled in the shower and began fondling each other, kissing each other hungrily.

"Man, that was a good session last night," Hank remarked.

"Yeah, looking forward to working that boy over some other time."

The two began scrubbing each other's backs. Fondling, hugging, and playing with each other's dicks.

"I want to fuck your ass," Hank started as he pulled on his own cock.

"Little time right now, handsome. We have to report by 6:45, remember?"

"Shit, that's right." The men finished their preparations and quickly put on their blue uniforms. The coffeemaker seemed to take forever to brew, but finally after downing two cups apiece, the men headed out for headquarters.

The captain always had a meeting first thing in the morning. Beat cops were normally apprised of any situations that had arisen the night before.

"Foley and Hernandez, you're gonna patrol the northeast sector today. Couple of punks terrorized an old lady last night. Stole her purse. Here's a description," the captain said as he handed them paperwork on the two thugs.

As Hank and Morris headed to the patrol car, Hank perused the info.

"Street punks, early 20s, one about 6 foot, the other shorter – about 5-7. Shaved heads. Tattoos on the forearms. Clothing sounds like skinhead gear."

"Good, sounds just like our type," Morris countered.

"Hope we meet up with them… although this description sounds like half the population of the city."

"The old lady had her rent money – $750 – in her purse. Here's a clue though, she had it all in large bills."

The cops quickly made their way through traffic to the northeast sector. A neighborhood filled with blue-collar workers. Decent hard-working people. A number of buildings boarded up. Graffiti and trash. The cops were used to it.

They parked the car and began canvassing the local grocery stores. Places that sold cigarettes. Liquor store. Lottery tickets. Nothing, no big bills had been used for the purchase of those goods. Or at least no one was saying anything if they knew. Afraid of retribution, probably.

After an hour and a half of not finding one single lead, the cops reconvened at the patrol car.

Hank lit a cigarette as he suggested searching some of the hangouts for local punks. Pool room. The local bars. The two stayed together this time but still got no solid leads. They headed to Roosevelt Park where punks congregated.

Hank spotted a group of young men congregated around a picnic table. As the cops approached the young men scattered, but the cops were intent on finding the culprits and pursued a couple of the guys.

Hernandez yelled for them to stop in Spanish. The guys just kept running, but Hank and Morris were both in good shape and soon outdistanced them. The boys reluctantly stopped.

"We didn't do nothing…"

"I didn't say you did; just want to ask you a few questions."

"What?" one of the guys said defiantly.

"We're looking for two punks who ripped off an old lady. Could have been your grandmother."

"We don't know 'em."

Hank was getting irritated, but Hernandez was more patient with the boys. It was obvious that these two – with curly black hair – weren't the punks in question, but might have heard on the street who was flashing big money this morning.

Morris proceeded to question the two in Spanish. They calmed down as they realized that they weren't the boys the cops were looking for.

After a few more questions, the cops realized that the boys didn't know, didn't care, just as long as it wasn't their asses that were in trouble.

"Let's come back here at night – we could probably pick up some good looking boys to fuck," Hank suggested.

"Your fucking mind is so concentrative on one thing, man-to-boy sex. Of course, I was thinking the same thing," Morris replied, giving his partner a thumbs up.

Hank and Morris reluctantly returned to the patrol car and drove to the old lady's address.

Knocking on her door, a curtain was pulled aside as the old lady peered nervously at them.

The cops showed their badges and she reluctantly opened the door.

"Ma'am, we're here to ask you a few questions about last night's robbery." She ushered them into her living room. It was obvious she was still pretty badly shaken, but having two strapping cops in your living room had a way of settling even the most frightened victim.

As they questioned her, she began crying. "What am I going to do? My rent is due today – I don't have any other place to live... they'll throw me out."

The cops reassured her that they would talk to her landlady as she handed over the landlady's telephone number and address to them.

Patting her on the shoulder and giving her a hug, the cops re-emerged from the woman's house. The landlady's house was only several blocks away and so, they marched down the street and knocked on her door.

The door was opened by a frail-looking woman with a look of fear on her face.

"Ma'am, we're here...," Morris started.

"He's not here. My nephew is not here..."

"Ma'am, we're here to ask..." Morris began again.

"I told you he is not here."

"Ma'am, let me finish. We are here to investigate a robbery that took place last night. Your tenant Rosa was robbed last night of her rent money."

"Oh, oh, I see." the lady quickly intoned.

The cops asked her a few questions, but both had picked up on the landlady's protective statements regarding her nephew and needed to pursue it.

"Question, Ma'am, where is your nephew if he is not here...?"

"Ahh, I don't know."

"Ma'am, withholding information from an officer of the law is subject to punishment."

The lady started crying, "All I know is Juan showed up at my door late last night around midnight. He and his friend Hector. High as kites – on drugs or booze, I don't know which.

He wanted to stay the night and I told him to get out. He started to threaten me and I grabbed my grandson's baseball bat from the dining room table and hit him... hit him in the head. God forgive me, but I was scared. He and Hector left. I bolted the door and prayed all night that he wouldn't return. That boy has a temper, especially when he's high like he was. God forgive me for that. I'm not going to be arrested, am I?"

"No, Ma'am, it's a clear case of self-defense. Now let me ask you a few more questions..."

At the end of the conversation, it was obvious that the two were quite possibly the same two that had stolen Rosa's money.

Finding them was another matter. Probably holed up somewhere, licking their wounds and nursing a bruise or a concussion to Juan's head.

"Let's check the clinic," Hank suggested as the men exited the house.

The two cops retrieved the patrol car and headed toward the medical clinic. While Morris drove, Hank cruised the people out on the streets. A normal day of activity.

"Hey, Morris, slow down... those two guys lounging in the doorway...," remarked Hank as he casually viewed them from behind his mirrored sunglasses.

"Fuck, man, that's gotta be them..." The two had already spotted the cop car and were making every effort to evaporate into the crowded streets.

Morris halted the car in the middle of the street and the cops hastily exited.

Their foot pursuit was soon rewarded as they spotted the two ducking into an alley.

As they entered the alley, there were numerous doorways. They had to try every door, but all that they tried were locked. The alley ended and the perps were not anywhere to be found. This led the cops to return to the front doors and inquire about the two. "No, don't know 'em," was the standard reply as the doors were hastily shut. The cops could hear deadbolts being thrown as they marched down the stoops.

As they retrieved their patrol car, Mo flatly stated, "Well, it looks as if they have won Round One. But now they know we're looking for them and they'll fuck up – sooner or later."

The cops returned to headquarters and reported their activities for the day. It was near quitting time, and the cops headed to Morris' house. They quickly stripped off their ass-tight blue uniforms and showered.

Both men couldn't wait to jam their ass in their Leathers and then mellow out with a glass of wine and a good, strong cigar. They wrestled on the floor, kissing, twisting each other's nips, massaging their mancocks, enjoying one another's homomasculinity.

"Let's head to Roosevelt Park," Mo suggested. The men retrieved their biker gear – heavy cycle jackets, shit-kicking engineer boots, and heavy gauntlets. Morris had been a biker for most of his life and his Harley stood gleaming in the garage, just ready for them to mount up and ride. Mo loaded a small bag of necessary supplies – bondage rope, handcuffs, duct tape, and gags, into the saddlebag.

They roared out of the driveway and headed for Roosevelt Park, usually alive with all sorts of illicit activity and usually a haven for handsome young hustlers.

The cops weren't disappointed. There were any number of young men enjoying the cool evening breeze.

Mo pulled out his cigar case and extracting two, handed one to his partner.

Each propped his booted foot against a sturdy tree, just looking and waiting. While they waited, they scoped out the surrounding area for a location removed from public view. It would be handy for the activity they anticipated.

Guys cruised by, but through a silent communication between the two cops, were rejected for one reason or another.

The cops watched and waited, dragging on their cigars, absently rubbing their increasingly-excited cocks through their Leathers.

"Mo, look at those two," whispered Hank.

Two guys had entered the park. They stood under the streetlamp, loudly talking to one another. Wearing their machismo on their muscled arms.

The two had their thumbs tucked into their faded jeans, bulging ass muscles filling out the faded jeans nicely. Their tee shirts were tucked into the back of their pants.

Nice nips. Handsome.

"Let's make our move," Mo suggested as he ambled slowly toward the two.

At first the young men didn't notice the Leathermen approaching. But, as the cops drew closer, the young men stood their ground.

"Evening," Mo nodded as he approached.

The two young men simply nodded.

"The park is crowded tonight – looks like you could get almost anything you want tonight...," Hank said in a suggestive tone.

The two young men simply acknowledged the statement with a shrug of their shoulders.

"Yep, for two guys who just got here, we were hoping for some action... and willing to pay," Mo said, as he pulled a few bills out of his breast pocket of his jacket. He continued to drag on his cigar.

The shorter of the two eyed Mo and Hank up and down. He was handsome. His pecs flexed as he pulled his hands out of his waistband and crossed them in front of his chest.

"You not from around here?"

"No," Mo said, convincingly, "we're just taking a road trip on my cycle. Meeting up with some Harley buddies in Washington State. We just wanted to stretch our legs for a while... release some of the, er, tension of the day" He reached down and absently rubbed his crotch. He looked off into the distance, eyeing the crowd. He knew he would pull these hustlers in if he continued to cruise, cruising for a better catch.

The other guy stepped forward, "We could help you release some of that tension, but it would cost you... $300 for the two of you."

"Well, now, that sounds reasonable. My buddy and I picked out a little area over here – out of sight, just in case we met up with two studs like you."

"Let's see your money first."

Mo presented the second hustler with the sheaf of bills. The guy carefully counted. "This is only $250."

"You haven't done anything for us yet."

"We want our money up front."

With that, Mo lost his temper, not unusual for him. Getting right up in the hustler's face, "Listen you punk, you'll get your fucking money after you've serviced me and not before." With that, he wrenched the hustler's arm behind his back. Hank did the same to the other hustler. Their forearms wrapped around the hustlers' throats, cutting off their air supply.

The hustlers put up resistance as the cops took them to the tree from which they had first observed the boys. With his arm still in a chokehold around the hustler's throat, Mo retrieved his bag of supplies and followed Hank as they maneuvered their new prey into the nearby woods.

Mo flattened his hustler to the tree with a body slam, facing the tree. The boy was squirming and as he started to yell, Mo stuffed the black bandana from his back pocket into the boy's mouth.

Hank had less trouble with the other hustler as he slammed the boy, face first, against a sturdy tree. A pair of handcuffs, extracted from his back pocket soon fastened the boy's arms around the tree. He too pulled a black bandana from his back pocket and tied it around the boy's mouth. He retrieved bondage rope from the bag of supplies and helped his partner secure Mo's fuckboy into place against the tree.

Reaching around, Mo roughly unzipped the tight jeans of his fuckboy. The jeans fell down to the boy's knees. A healthy cock and balls were revealed. He manhandled the cock with his gloved hand while rubbing the boy's back with his other gloved hand. The boy put up a violent struggle until Mo was forced to slap him across the cheek. Once, twice, three times until Mo lost count. That settled the boy momentarily. He unzipped his Leather jacket and pressed his man nips against the boy's back. He began rubbing the boy's back. Despite the boy's resistance or fear, this action seemed to calm him down. Mo continued to stroke the boy's cock until it was hardened and pressed against the rough bark of the tree.

Both cops could feel their manjuices gathering in their cockshafts as they unzipped their Leather pants. Their cocks sprang forward.

As if in synchronized motion, the men lubed up their extended rods with spit and eased their cocks up the receptive holes of their two new victims.

"Fuck, bro, this feels good," Hank remarked.

Mo was leaning forward, slowly pumping his cock's head into the boy's hole. His back and head were arched backward as the thrusts became more violent. He held onto the boy's ribcage as he continued to thrust his manrod into the boy's healthy ass.

He reached around and began squeezing the boy's nips. Hank duplicated the actions – holding onto the boy's tits with an iron grip.

Mo's boy was still squirming, but Hank's boy was apparently enjoying the fucking. He began to moan softly as Hank's cock made its way up his chute.

The two men continued pumping, edging their cocks out, playing with their juiced-up rods, and re-inserting them.

Each cop pulled out a small bottle of poppers from their cycle jacket pockets and after taking a hit themselves, made their boys take several hits. Their masculine bodies pressed hard against the young men's captive bodies.

"I want to prolong this, bro," Mo moaned, "but my cock is ready to pump." He squeezed his cock hard, hoping to soften it. It did just the opposite, a few drops of precum appeared in the slit.

He guided his cock back into the boy's fuck chute and began a frenzied pumping. Within minutes, he shot a load of cum.

Hank controlled his load better, but still came within a few minutes after his partner, whispering, "Fuck!" as he came.

All four were sweating, the boys were breathing heavily.

Mo finally extracted his cock from the boy's ass. The night was not over yet. He marched over to the bag and extracted a small, but effective flogger. He began whipping the boy's ass and back with it. An experienced flogger, Mo soon had the boy's back covered in lash marks. The young hustler twisted and turned within his bondage ropes, but there was to be no release. Mo checked on the boy's cock and found it pulsing with cum. He grabbed it with his Leather gloved hand and despite the grimace on the boy's face, his teeth gritted against the bandana, he shot a load against the tree. "Aahhh!" the boy shouted, muffled by the gag.

Hank withdrew his swollen cock and began to work on his boy's nips. They were already erect as he pulled and pinched on them. The boy's cock was pressed against the tree. Hank began slapping the boy's asscheeks with his gloved hands and the boy shot a load against the tree.

"Good boys," Mo remarked as he caught the defiant eyes of his victim.

He pulled on the boy's tits as he taunted, "You ready to be fucked again?"

He lathered up his right glove with a bottle of lube extracted from the zippered pocket of his cycle jacket. His fingers tickled the recently-explored hole of the boy fucked by Hank. The boy seemed willing to take his fist as he arched his ass.

Hank greased up his gloved hand, trading places with his partner. Boy No. #1's ass was clenched tight, but a few sharp slaps of the Leather gloved hands of Hank loosened up the boy's fisting hole. Hank eased his fingers up the boy's butt and fisted him with little more resistance.

The fisting only aroused the two cops. Finally removing his fist from Boy #2's butt, Mo began a concentrated flogging of the boy's back, shoulders, ribcage, and ass.

The boy's back looked like an erotic road map of S&M destinations.

Mo stood back momentarily to admire his own work. He fondled his cock into hardness. Marching over to Boy #2, he slid it easily up the stretched hole.

While Hank was fisting his captive, he worked on his own cock. It was responding nicely and was soon hard enough to seek another hole. What better choice than Boy #1. He slid his cock into place and the scene began all over again.

It didn't take either cop long before they shot their cum up the boys' captive chutes.

"Fuck, yeah!" Mo sighed as he shot.

"Fuck, bro! That was some good pussy we just got," Hank observed.

Their cocks dripping, the two cops stood back to admire their work.

"Oh, bro, forgot one thing…," Mo said as he sauntered over to the boy who had pocketed his money. He reached into the boy's tight jeans, now around his knees, and extracted a wad of bills. His fingers wrapped around a plastic bag, which he took without looking.

Before releasing the boys, the two cops removed the boys' boots and jeans. They placed them a good distance away.

They unhandcuffed Hank's boy and removed the bondage rope from Mo's boy. The two boys slumped to the ground. Hank retrieved the black bandanas and the cops, gathering up their supplies and tool bag, hastily departed.

Hopping on their Harley, they left Roosevelt Park and two cum-filled hustlers.

The two cops arrived back at Mo's house. They remained in their Leathers as they mellowed out with cigars and drinks.
They settled on the sofa and clicked on the local news.
They began heavy petting, fondling each other's cock and balls through their Leather pants and pretty soon, the pants were open and the cocks were being treated to a Leather gloved massage. Fucking captive boys just made them hornier.

"Fuck, bro. That felt so good, working over those two. Wish we had gotten their names..." Hank remarked as he chuckled at his own joke.

"I dare say they'll stay clear of the park for a while. Especially if they see a cycle park near it," as Morris joined in the joke.

He reached in his pocket and extracted the thick wad of cash. "Fuck, bro, there's other a thousand bucks here... those boys were busy tonight. Look what else I retrieved," he said, as he pulled out the plastic bag. "A good supply of weed for me and my partner to enjoy." There were carefully-rolled joints.

"Ah, Mo, you ruined their party... you big insensitive fucker," Hank replied as he leaned over and stuck his tongue down his partner's throat.

CHAPTER 3

Gym Rats

The following day was a rare day off for the two cops. They slept in late, fucked in bed, enjoyed their morning coffee out on the patio, and then fucked again. It was a spectacular day – sunny, but not too hot. In the late afternoon, the guys suited up and headed to the gym.

They stowed their gear in their lockers and headed for the weight room. Some of the regulars were already there, pumping. Hank did a quick cruise around the room to see if there was any fresh meat. He was slightly disappointed that there was not. But the day was still young.

The guys worked up a good sweat as they did their rotations on the machines. After a good two and a half hours, they hit the showers.

They stood in opposite corners of the shower; the gym was not a bathhouse after all. Even though they both wanted to fuck one another that would come later.

Morris stood a little over six foot. He was a man who had always taken care of his body. Now in his late 40s, he did not exhibit the middle-aged sag that so many men of his age experienced. His hair was black, with touches of grey at the temples. His brown eyes could bore into the center of someone's brain when he was asking a question. Nice pecs, the kind you want to grab a handful of as soon as you saw them. Moderately hairy, with a furline leading right down to the family jewels. His cock was short and thick – his balls hung low, from years of playing with stretchers and from years, of well, playing.

As he enjoyed the warmth of the shower's pulsating water, he looked over to his partner.

"Fuck, you are attractive. I'd try to pick you up if we weren't already together."

Hank was a half-inch shorter than Mo and five years younger. His hairline was just showing signs that it might recede. In his day, his hair was a crop of blonde hair, but it had started to turn greyish white. He kept it shaved in a military cut. Strong facial bones, making him look more like a medieval warrior. Handsome chest. A fine blonde fur covered his body. Only the pubic hair surrounding his handsome, veined dick was dark. His balls hung low too – he attributed it to pulling on them so much in his early jack-off days. And there had been a lot of them! The guys who had seen Hank's ass agreed that he had a perfect ass. Many guys had tried but only Mo had succeeded in spreading those cheeks and inserting his cock.

Hank had joined the police force seven years after Morris and was immediately taken by the handsome patrol cop he was paired off with. It wasn't long after the two were paired that Morris pulled the patrol car off to the side of the road, pulled Hank's face toward him, and rammed his tongue down Hank's throat.

"I don't care if you are gay or not," Morris panted, "I just had to do that."

"Why did you stop?" Hank said, as he pulled Morris' mouth toward his.

After duty that night, the two went back to Hank's apartment and fucked like animals. They had been together ever since.

The hot water served as a stimulant and the guys were soon sporting boners. Nowhere to hide those when you're standing in a shower, naked.

As the water continued to pulsate against their skin, the two were mutually thinking of the session that had taken place the night before. The cocks got even harder.

Out of the corner of his eye, Hank saw a guy stripping in front of a locker and he soon paddled into the shower area.

The guys nodded to him and a knowing look crossed their brief eye contact.

"Fuck," Hank thought, "would I enjoy planting my seed in that ass." Mo was thinking the same thing.

The guy was handsome. Muscular. Trim waist, broad shoulders. Hung like a fucking horse. Young, mid-twenties or so. Blonde hair, blue eyes.

The guy began soaping his chest, slathering it on. Rubbing his genitals with the bar of soap.

He finally spoke to them, in an Australian accent, "Hey, guys. This gym is top rate. Didn't think I would get such a good workout."

Mo replied, "Yeah, it's well-stocked. You're not from around here, are you?"

The newcomer replied, "Now, how did you know that?"

"Well, I detect a slight accent."

"I'm Chris. In the states on assignment from 'Down Under'."

"I'm Morris – this is my buddy Hank."

"Nice to meet you, mates. Looks like you work out often."

"We do our best," Hank said coyly.

"Damned good looking men, I have to say."

"You ain't bad yourself, mate."

The guy was rinsing himself off and the guys instantly knew that they only had a few moments to capture this handsome lad.

"Hank and I were gonna go out for a couple of drinks afterward – want to join us?"

"Sure, mate."

The guys toweled off, dressed, and exited the gym. The men led the young man to a bar several blocks away.

As they settled down to drinks, Chris revealed more details of his work.

"What do you guys do?"

"We're cops."

"Oh, that must be exciting work..."

"It has its moments, mate."

Chris further revealed his work would keep him in the States for three months, but the guys were thinking ahead only to later that same night.

"Your wife is gonna miss you, Buddy. Or did you bring her along?"

"I don't have a wife. My partner and I have been together for four years."

A knowing look crossed the cops' eyes.

"Oh, so, you left him in the hotel room?" Hank innocently asked.

"No, nothing like that. He couldn't get away..."

"Oh, pity...," said Hank sympathetically.

"Say, Buddy, why don't you come back to our place for a good cigar..."

"Damn, mate, thought you'd never ask."

The three men left the bar. He retrieved his rental car and followed the Harley back to Morris' house.

"Nice place," Chris commented as he viewed some of the erotic Leather artwork on the living room walls. He had carried a small bag into the house.

"Mind if I change into something more comfortable, mates?" Chris asked.

"Sure, Buddy, make yourself at home." Mo answered as he hastened to the kitchen to fix drinks and Hank went to retrieve cigars.

Only a few minutes later, when they returned to the living room, Chris had stripped down to a Leather jockstrap, gloves, and a bullwhip.

"Thought you guys might be into Leather...," he calmly stated.

"Yes, but we have a problem here. We're both tops."

"No problem, mate. I want you to use it on me," Chris responded, as he held up the bullwhip.

"Fuck, bro. I can't believe our luck."

The two men repaired to the upstairs and quickly shed their workout clothing, replacing them with boots, chaps, and their executioners' hoods.

They escorted the young man downstairs, where he willingly stood in front of the St. Andrew's Cross. He was manacled into place. They placed a Leather hood over his handsome face.

Mo explained that they would warm him up with their own floggers before using the bullwhip on his muscular back.

Endless rotations with their heaviest floggers took place, all without the boy once flinching. His muscular back and firm ass flexed occasionally, otherwise he stood calmly, never crying out, seeming to enjoy it all.

Morris and Hank both offered encouragement during the extended session and asked the boy if he was okay.

"Fine, Sir. Thank you, Sir," was Chris' standard reply.

Morris retrieved the bullwhip, which was tightly furled. It would take a little practice to execute the whipping. Both men had used a bullwhip, but usually in an outdoor setting. Some underhand swings caught the boy's asscheeks. Overhand swings got caught in the rafters of the basement playroom. Finally, Mo perfected a sideways strike, which evenly distributed the lashes on the boy's willing back and ass. He lighted a big fucker of a cigar, clenching it firmly between his jaw.

"CRACK!" "CRACK!" "CRACK!" as welts began to appear on the boy's frame. He still stood calmly.

With a little more wrist action, Mo began snapping the bullwhip expertly, the single tail catching the boy on the shoulder blades, ribcage, and asscheeks. The blood was quickly rising to the surface as the executioners took turns. Finally, trails of blood were crisscrossing the boy's back. The boy still stood calmly, not flinching when the single tail bit into his flesh.

The two cops rotated, their cocks hardening. And the single-tail whipping continued. This boy was expert at being a pain pig. The two cops wanted to take full advantage of the opportunity.

"CRACK!" "CRACK!" The fucking bullwhip seemed to smoke with each new lash, as the boy's back was increasingly a landscape of blood.

After a length of time, the two men couldn't control their manjuices any longer. Both cocks were dripping precum.

They took the boy down from the St. Andrew's Cross and forced him to kneel.

Hank guided his cock into the boy's mouth and the boy vacuumed the cock until it was dry. Hank's cum was relished and swallowed. In short order, he had sucked Morris dry too.

"Damn, boy. That is the best cocksucking I've had..." Hank said, slightly awestruck.

"I'm glad you liked it, Sir."

Morris thanked him as well. They escorted him upstairs and treated his back with antiseptic.

"I am truly impressed, son. I've never seen anyone take a whipping like that."

"Well, Sir, my partner and I have been practicing for some time. You may have heard of him, actually, he's Lord Aussie."

"Fuck? The porn star?" Hank exclaimed.

"No other. I've been in some of the films too. Actually, he's due to arrive in three weeks to discuss an American film deal. As I leave, he'll be arriving." The boy revealed more details of the impending film deal, which would bring Lord Aussie to Dallas – not all that far away from the horny cops. And plans were already swirling around in the separate brains of the cops before the boy said another word.

"Well, son, a pleasure to have you here."

That was the young man's cue that the night was winding up. He flashed a generous smile as he said, "Yes, I better get going. If you can direct me back to the hotel."

"You're welcome to spend the night," Morris offered.

"Tell you what, mates, I'd like to come back if you'd have me. That whipping felt so damned good, I felt right at home," as he laughed, "but I've got an early morning meeting at the hotel and so, better go back now."

The two cops assured him that he was welcome in their house any time, like every night for the next three months, and reluctantly sent him on his way. As it turned out, the boy returned for two more sessions before heading back to Australia.

"Damn, partner, that was great," said Hank as the two retired for the evening.

CHAPTER 4

Capturing the Punks

The two men woke the next morning to a steady drizzle of rain. It was hard climbing out of their warm nest of naked flesh and mansex. They slowly got ready and arrived at headquarters only a few moments before the captain called his daily meeting to order. The captain had a suppressed smile on his face, which usually meant good news for his department. The captain was unselfish in his devotion to the department and the men who staffed it. Before imparting any good news, the news of the night had to be shared first.

"Okay, guys, here's the assignments for the day...," the captain read a long roster, finally getting to Hernandez and Foley.

"Yesterday and overnight, we had two more robberies... old ladies... their purses. Everybody knows its social security check time. Probably the same perps who you investigated, guys. Go back... find the dirtbags." The guys nodded acceptance for the challenge.

The captain continued his list of projects to completion.

"And now, men, some really good news to share with you. It will change our department into a more effective, aggressive fighting mechanism without our community. We have been awarded $300,000 for the purchase of motorcycles for a mounted patrol division." The guys cheered at the announcement.

"Ten cycles. And to head up the unit I am appointing Officer Hernandez to head the unit." Mo's jaw dropped, as the guys continued to cheer the appointment. The captain continued, "I can't think of anyone more qualified – I think Mo was on a cycle with training wheels before he could walk. Mo and I will confer on the other patrolmen to join the motorcycle unit."

The little kid in Hank wanted to jump up and down and yell, "Pick Me! Pick Me!" but simply slapped his partner on the back along with the other guys. He knew Mo would remain faithful to their partnership even if he wasn't one of the others picked.

The announcement having been made, the cops dispersed to their assigned duties for the day.

After an initial conference with the captain, Hernandez returned to his patrol car where Hank was patiently waiting.

The guys once again headed out to the northeast sector, more determined than ever to pick up the scumbags that had targeted old ladies. A steadier rain was falling, making visibility less than perfect. Hank cruised the streets as Morris drove. The police reports detailed the robbers, who were becoming bolder in their actions. Both purse-snatchings had occurred during the daylight hours. The physical descriptions matched the same punks who had stolen Rosa's money.

The cops interviewed the two frightened women, who confirmed the physical descriptions presented to the cops. Both had received their social security checks and had recently cashed them to pay bills. A pattern was emerging with the information that all three victims were tenants of Juan's aunt.

"You don't think she's in on it, do you?" Hank questioned.

"No, but she may be feeding them the info by being careless about her record-keeping. Let's go pay Mrs. DeLa Rosa another visit," Mo answered.

This time there was no response to the repeated knockings at her door.

The cops questioned a few of the neighbors. Only one neighbor remembers having seen her. She was leaning into the window of a car parked near her house.

The car, as described by the witness, was an older model of a Lincoln Town Car.

Hernandez radioed in the information and was soon rewarded with a Town Car registered to Hector Juarez, aged thirty-three. A further report revealed that Hector had been in and out of jail for distribution with intent to sell various illegal drugs, theft, forgery, and the list continued.

"I think we have our perps...," Morris concluded.

The cops cruised around but did not spot a Lincoln among all the many parked vehicles in the surrounding neighborhoods.

A further investigation revealed that Hector's sister, who had signed several of his bail bonds, lived close by. "Let's pay her a visit," Hank suggested, as the patrol car headed to the street on which she lived.

The sister quickly denied having seen her brother in weeks, but her eyes shifted nervously away from Mo's steady stare.

"Ma'am," Hank said softly, "withholding evidence is punishable by the law. Just as bad as robbing an old lady of her Social Security money."

The young woman started fidgeting with the collar of her blouse.

"All right," she said finally, "Hector was here this morning. He left a small bag of clothing and said he would be back this afternoon to pick it up."

"Get it," Mo ordered, tiring of the games he had to play with loyal relatives and friends of punks.

As the cops sifted through the bag of clothing, their trained eyes looking for evidence, they discovered a false bottom to the bag. Underneath was a large amount of cash and a quantity of pot.

Mo wrote a receipt for the bag of clothing and handing it to her, asked, "What time did he say he would come back?"

She hesitated, but looking up at the big beefy cops, she half-whispered, "Four thirty."

"Ma'am, we will be back. You are to say nothing to Hector if he calls or contacts you," Mo sternly warned her, "If you do, you will be going to jail along with them."

She began crying as they left and re-entered their patrol car.

The two cops devised a plan, which would require a hasty return to Mo's house.

When the cops arrived back at the sister's house, it was a little after four. The men were now dressed in black Leather. Morris' cycle was parked several doors away from the sister's house. The cops' identification badges were tucked safely away in their cycle jacket pockets. Hank carried a small Leather bag filled with necessary supplies for the take-down. As a precaution, the cops both put on executioner's hoods to disguise their features.

And they were no disappointed. At 4:25, a Lincoln Town Car pulled up to the sister's house and the two punks, matching the descriptions, emerged. They looked hastily to the left and to the right, before taking the steps up to the house two at a time. What they failed to view was two men, in full Leather, discreetly hidden behind the bushes flanking the steps.

"Hector, is that you?" Morris called, in Spanish. As Hector and Juan looked to see where the voices had come from, two Leathermen jumped from opposite directions and quickly restrained the arms of the punks behind their backs.

"What the fuucck?" Hector yelled as a black Leather glove clamped over his mouth. The two began to struggle as the larger of the men put a chokehold around both their throats. The other Leatherman quickly secured duct tape around each of the punks' ankles. They struggled as they were dragged down the steps and thrown in the back of the Lincoln town car. Duct tape was wrapped around their mouths and over their eyes and then added around their upper arms. The capture was done in a matter of minutes, without seeming notice of anyone in the neighborhood. A steadier rain was falling and most people had retreated inside. A curtain drawn to one side at the sister's house revealed Hector's sister, crying as she saw her brother taken away by two men in black.

Alarmed, she telephoned the police station and asked to speak to Officer Hernandez.

Hank extracted the car keys from Hector's pocket and climbed into the driver's seat.

The Lincoln had an unofficial police escort as a Harley pulled away from the curb. The punks were taken to an unofficial interrogation room at Morris' house.

Hank kept up a steady barrage of taunts, disguising his voice, all the way back to the dungeon. He wanted the young fuckers to be feisty. All the better to work them over.

They were kicking the back of the seat. Cursing at him through the duct tape. Squirming. He just hoped that the duct tape would hold until they got back to the dungeon.

The drive seemed to take forever – Morris had to slow his Harley because the rain was pelting him and he didn't want to risk an accident even though his cock was throbbing anxiously against its' Leather enclosure. "Keep your mind focused," he kept telling himself, "don't think with your cock yet."

As he pulled into the driveway of his den of iniquity, he sighed a sigh of relief. He opened the second garage door for Hank to pull in the Lincoln. He and Hank pulled Hector out first and escorted him down the steps into the dungeon. The boy was struggling and was quite strong. He was screaming behind the duct tape. As Hank strapped the boy down to the workover table, Morris retrieved the black Leather hood that had proved so useful in the past. It was quickly placed over Hector's head. As they placed it firmly over Hector's nostrils, Hank ripped off the duct tape – a good deal of Hector's pencil-thin mustache hairs coming with it. Hector started screaming as they laced the hood into place and a plug placed in the boy's mouth.

The two cops hastened back to the car only to find Juan in the process of wiggling out of the car. How he thought he would get anywhere with duct tape around his ankles and arms amused the cops, who quickly grabbed him under the arms and dragged him down the steps. He was soon secured to the black Leather sling with wrist and ankle restraints. His face was also hooded and his screaming was soon quelled with a plug in his mouth. The two cops tested the restraints before retreating upstairs.

Morris toweled off his wet Leathers. He was soaked from the rain. The telephone was blinking as he retrieved the messages of the day. One call was from Headquarters, indicating that Hector's sister had witnessed her brother and his friend being forced into his Lincoln. Headquarters asked Mo to call back.

"Okay, I'll call her... yeah, we were supposed to, but the patrol car broke down on us and we never got there... Engine trouble. Yeah, it's fixed for the moment," Mo explained, in a convincing voice.

He called Hector's sister and told her that he and Officer Foley would be over as soon as possible to take down details about the abduction.

"Well, handsome, the trophies have arrived," Mo explained hastily, "but Hector's sister witnessed the trophy taking. We'd better haul ass before any suspicions arise."

First checking that the punks were securely restrained, the cops headed upstairs and exchanged their Leathers for their uniforms.

"It'll give them a little time to settle down," Morris suggested.

"Fuck, I want to work them both over... the arrogant pieces of shit. I want to abuse the two muthafuckers," Hank remarked as he lit a cigarette. He handed one to his partner.

"Calm down, your horny fucker. We got them as long as we want..." The two cops laughed.

Morris pressed his body against his partner's handsome body. Their cocks, still encased in Leather jocks, were pressing against each other's.

Their lips met as Hank pulled his partner's head toward his.

Their tongues explored each other's mouths. The two Leathermen kissed for a long time, fondling each other's bodies. Their ass muscles pulled in tight, cocks thrust forward and arm muscles flexing.

"Damn, Hank, I want to fuck you..."

"I want to taste your cock..."

"Better go... we have plenty of time to fuck when we get back..."

The two cops hastened to the 'scene of the crime' and filled out an investigative report. The sister was crying but was reassured by Hank, who said, "We'll find them."

He winked at his partner. They knew exactly where the fuckers were.

Arriving back home, the two cops headed upstairs and quickly shed their cop clothing. Their Leathers were once again put on, in anticipation of the sex scene that was about to take place – two willing, two not-so-willing.

Hornier than ever at the deed they had accomplished, the two remained upstairs for several more minutes as they proceeded to suck each other. Their cocks were fully engorged with mancum as the cocks pulsated in each other's mouth. Their masculine Leathered bodies rubbing against one another. Heads bobbing up and down on swollen cocks. Gloved hands rubbing. Cumming in each other's mouth. Kissing, taste of a man's own cum in his mouth.

"Damn! That felt good...," Hank said as he faced his partner, "but I'm anxious to work over those boys, aren't you?"

Morris kissed his partner, "You know I can't wait – I'm as horny as you are, you bastard."

The two men placed their executioners' hoods on and went downstairs.

CHAPTER 5

Taming

The two Leathermen entered the dungeon. The two captive boys were both violently struggling and pulling against the restraints that held them firmly in place. They were violently shaking their heads from side to side, moaning, and cursing as much as one could with a plug in your mouth.

The two Leathermen watched in amused detachment. "Pretty soon, boys," Hank thought, "you'll have more to worry about than the restraints you are in."

Both men sauntered over to the two captives.

Morris took the lead, bellowing, "PRISONERS, you have been brought here to be punished. Abused. Brutalized. Terrorized. Sodomized. You are now the prisoners of two men who enjoy inflicting pain on other human beings – specifically young men, of legal age, who have been bad and need to be taught a lesson. What's the lesson you are to learn? Treat other human beings as you wish to be treated and since you terrorized old ladies, we're going to show you what we do to cowards like you who prey on innocent people. You have treated them like shit and now, it's your turn to be treated like SHIT." With that pronouncement, Morris stood beside Hector and Hank stood beside Juan and delivered doubled up fists to the offenders' privates. The scream that escaped from beneath the Leather hoods was the first of many.

Morris was angry that these two pieces of human garbage would terrorize an old lady. With one powerful jerk, he ripped off the cheap tee shirt Hector wore. He unzipped Hector's pants, hoping that he would catch Hector's privates in the zipper, but Hector had on tidy whities. With the help of the sharpened knife on Morris' belt, they were ripped off as well. Leaving the boy naked and vulnerable. Hank followed suit and soon the two boys were naked except for their boots. Both boys were shivering. As well, they should be.

Morris leaned down into Hector's face, making eye contact with Hector as he said, "You disgust me, you are human garbage." As he was saying this, he poised the knife in front of Hector's frightened eyes.

"You coward, I ought to cut your balls off right now...." as he reached down with the knife and flicked the left ball with the knife blade, "Maybe just one..."

An audible "No" was heard behind the hood, followed by a violent shaking of the head. The boy tried to cover his balls with his thighs.

Morris crawled on top of the boy and held the knife to Hector's sternum. "Maybe I should just slice you right down the center... see if you have a yellow streak down your back, you fucking asshole." The boy was apparently terrorized and was shaking violently.

Morris grabbed him by the top of the hood, "You ever do anything like this again, I'll find you, boy. I'm gonna strip your hide tonight, but if you ever do anything like this again, I will strip you down to the fucking bone." And with that, Morris pulled the heaviest Leather flogger – a flogger with no mercy and proceeded to give one hundred of the heaviest lashes he had ever inflicted on a boy. On his chest, his ribcage, his arms and shoulders, even between his legs. Morris' anger was intensifying as the boy's body became a mass of red streaks.

Hank was no less incensed by Juan, who was also straining against his manacles and shaking his head. He was just less vocal about it. Hank began slapping the boy's hooded face with the flattened palms of his black Leather gloved hands. The boy attempted to wrench his face away from the slaps, but Hank's hand made contact each and every time.

Standing beside the sling, Hank delivered a series of hard slaps to the boy's ribcage, his chest, and the boy's shriveled cock.

"You muthafucker, get that dick hard," Hank warned as he continued to slap the boy's frightened cock.

Leaning down into the boy's face, Hank yelled, "Get that dick hard, I want something that I can torture, you fucking prick."

The boy's cock remained flaccid. Hank delivered a series of gut punches. "I'll show you who's the man around here, you fucking pussy."

Juan was moaning, shaking his head from side to side.

Hank stepped away from the sling, retrieving one of the many floggers the cops had in their collection. He began flogging the boy's shoulders and ribcage. The Leather straps cut into the boy's slender frame and soon produced a series of red welts.

Hank reached up and twisted the boy's virgin nips. The boy wrenched in his restraints as the vise-like clamp of Hank's powerful hands twisted and pulled. Despite his fear, Juan's dick began to swell.

"Well, we finally have found your on-off controls, pussy boy," Hank observed. With that, he pulled a pair of alligators from his pocket and attached them. The clamps bit into the boy's tender titflesh. Yet another scream was heard from behind the hood.

"Next stage, boy," Hank informed the captive as he greased up his right hand and inserted it up the boy's rectum. The boy wrenched from the pain inflicted on his virgin hole.

Hank's hand wiggled further and further until his hand had disappeared and only his wrist was visible.

"This is what it feels like when your boyfriend in prison pleasures himself... on a daily basis," Hank taunted, as he laughed sadistically, "Just giving you a taste of what's to come, boy. My hole-stretching is free of charge, boy."

With less difficulty this time, Morris flipped his captive over on the workover table. Some of the boy's feistiness had been drained out of him.

Morris re-secured the boy face down. The boy's ass was so inviting, but Morris wanted to first warm the boy up. With the same flogger, he inflicted one hundred lashes on the boy's back and ass.

"CRACK! CRACK!" went the flogger as it met with fresh terrain to mark. Morris' cock was pounding in its cod. He showed no mercy as the flogger continued to make its' mark on the boy's tender flesh.

The boy was soon covered in bloody streaks left from the flogger's sadistic Leather tails.

Periodically, Morris stood back to admire his work and massage his own erect cock. It was telling Morris that it needed pleasuring too and that desire would soon be met.

After the 100 lashes, Morris climbed onto the worktable, straddling the boy's spread legs. With his greased up gloves, he roughly fingered the boy's hole, spreading the asscheeks. He unsnapped his cod and his hardened cock sprang forward.

He lubed the cock with his greased up gloved hands and rammed the cock up the boy's hole. The boy had been moaning during the lashings, his moans now turned to screams as Morris' healthy example of manhood made its way up the boy's hole. It glided into place as if it had visited the hole before.

Morris pulled the boy's head backward and hissed, "Enjoying it, boy?" The boy just screamed.

"That's all you can say, fuckboy? You should be grateful that you have Daddy's cock up your ass." He released the boy's head, which landed with a thud on the table.

"Ungrateful boy," Morris concluded.

As his cock thrust back and forth in the boy's hole, Morris reached into his jacket and pulled out a cigar. He had already clipped it and so, lighted it and took a deep draw on it while fucking the boy's ass. He looked over to Hank and the men exchanged smiles of contented pleasure.

Hank finally withdrew his fist. He pulled the boy's body toward the bottom of the sling.

His Leather gloved hand stroked his cock as he pulled it out of his cod. It was pulsing with the anticipated pleasure of fucking a stretched asshole.

His cock entered the boy's hole and seemed to double in size as it inched up the boy's rectum.

Hank began a slow and steady thrusting. He too reached into his cigar pouch and extracted a cigar. He drew on it deeply as he continued to thrust his cock into the boy's ass.

Both men wanted to prolong their pleasuring and so, would edge their cocks to readiness and then pull it out. A few minutes of concentrated smoking and then the cocks would be re-inserted for maximum enjoyment.

"Fuck, bro, we need music to accompany this…" Hank joked.

"You want me to sing?" Mo asked.

"Hell, no. That would make my cock shrink," Hank replied.

"Fuck you, bitch," Mo said to his partner.

And the two men continued.

The cops mutually liked virgin ass to fuck. It was pleasurable to have a mission as well. Teach these boys a lesson. Of course, even if they didn't have the mission, it still would have been good fucking.

The cops continued to control their hardened cocks as they enjoyed smoking their cigars. The boys had ceased moaning and screaming. The cops had worn them down.

The boys' holes were prepared for similar invasions and Hank thought momentarily of keeping the two boys as slaves. "We can't keep them indefinitely," he rationalized, "they are felons. Of course, they could just disappear off the face of the earth... who the fuck would care?" He finally concluded that family members would, as he ramped up his cock thrusting.

The two Leathermen retreated upstairs while their victims lay motionless, worn out from the extended abuse served up to them by two sadists.

As the two Leather cops lighted fresh cigars, they discussed the return of the two punks.

"Let's give them a day or two to think about the experience. They should be easy to pick up after this session," Hank suggested.

"Yeah, if we hauled their asses to the headquarters tonight. They might put two and two together."

At 3 am, the two Leathermen, still dressed in full Leather, entered the dungeon. The two punks were silent, apparently dozing after their night of brutality.

They were tightly wrapped in bondage rope, with duct tape over their mouth and eyes. Putting them back in the Lincoln Town Car was a much easier task. The two cops reversed the pattern, Hank pulling out in the Town Car. Mo waited five minutes or so before heading out as well. The neighborhood was dark, most people having retreated for the night to the relative safety of their homes, deadbolts in place. Word of the abduction had spread quickly but no one was overly concerned. Just two punks, low lifes, thieves, preying on innocent old ladies, probably beaten up and robbed of their ill-gotten money. Only the few friends and relatives that Juan and Hector had were concerned. Only Hector's sister remained faithful. She sat by the window, praying the rosary for Hector's safe return. She had cried until she was out of tears. She fell asleep in her chair near the window, her head drooping forward.

She woke as the sun shone brightly through the lace curtain. She pulled it aside. Hector's Town Car was parked near the front of her house. She rushed out of her house in her bathrobe. Hector was doubled up in the front seat of his car. He was shirtless with bloodied marks covering his chest and back. Duct tape covered his mouth and eyes, but she could see he was breathing steadily. Juan was in the back seat in a similar situation. With a great deal of difficulty, she escorted the young men into her house. She questioned them in disjointed Spanish and English but the two did not have much to say. She called the police station and asked for Officer Hernandez.

Officers Hernandez and Foley appeared several hours later and questioned the two men, filling out an incident report. At the same time, he served Warrants for the arrest of the two – on suspicion of robbery. The two were led in handcuffs to the Headquarters and later remanded to the County Jail. It was only a matter of time before the three trembling victims were brought into the station for positive identifications. Maybe prison life would settle them down – at least they had been prepped for their future roles as inmates' bitches.

CHAPTER 6

Marcus

In his rearview mirror, Marcus saw the motorcycle cops put on their flashing lights and blaring sirens. "They'll get around me any minute," Marcus thought.

They didn't. Instead, one of the cops motioned for Marcus to pull his Mercedes to the shoulder. He didn't immediately comply. The cop continued to point to the shoulder of the road.

Marcus reluctantly pulled over. As he reluctantly eased his wallet out of his tight-assed jeans, he wondered what infraction he had committed.

Both the motorcycle cops dismounted their cycles and marched toward Marcus' car window. He viewed them in his rear view mirror. Both beefy men. Tight blue uniform revealing muscular chests and thighs. Tight black Leather gloves and knee-high black boots. Mirrored sunglasses. "Woof," Marcus thought silently. One cop approached the car while the other observed from the trunk of Marcus' car, his hand poised near his gun's holster.

Despite Marcus' uncertainty, his member started to rise in his jeans.

Marcus nodded as he said, "Good morning, officer." As the officer leaned down, he removed the mirrored sunglasses. A handsome pair of eyes were capped with black eyebrows and lashes. The officer's sideburns had some grey streaked throughout. The officer rested his gloved hands on the car doorframe.

"Let me see your driver's license and registration card."

Marcus handed over the documents, including his passport, visa, and the rental agreement from the leasing company. He asked, "Was I doing something wrong?"

"Routine check. We're searching for a stolen Mercedes, which fits the description of your vehicle. Yours is a leased vehicle, huh? Oh, I see here you're from Australia. Are you in the country for pleasure or business?"

"I'm here on business."

"Well, the documents match up. Sorry to have bothered you, Mr. Douglas."

As he returned the documents to Marcus, the cop's eyes lingered, making eye contact a little longer than necessary. Mo quickly took in the swollen package inside the handsome man's pants. And he was handsome. An easy smile. Honey brown eyes with a golden brown shade of hair. The young man was muscular. His unbuttoned shirt revealed two pecs with that same golden brown hair. One muscle in particular held Mo's interest.

Marcus wanted to prolong the conversation and so quickly said, "Aah, officer. I'm not familiar with the restaurants in this area – can you recommend one?" It was approaching the noon hour and Marcus had an appointment at two.

The officer once again leaned down, his arms flexing as he once again gripped the doorframe with his gloved hands. His steady gaze was emotionless, but in his head, Mo was undressing the boy.

"Ah, yeah, five miles up this pike, take the Exit for Wentworth. Follow it to the first lighted intersection. Make a left, two stop signs, and then take a right. The Long Horn Diner is on the left. Best damned chili on the planet – guaranteed to put hair on your chest," as the cop winked at him.

Marcus couldn't help but notice the black fur that appeared above the cop's white tee shirt and on his arms. It caused him to remark, "Well, officer, then you must eat there quite often!"

"My partner and I were headed there for our lunch break – you can follow us – join us – if you like." Mo knew that he had hooked the boy; it was just a matter of pulling him in.

"Will do," Marcus replied, "Thanks, I'm Marcus," as he stuck his hand out of the window.

"I'm Morris – most people call me Mo," as Morris gripped the boy's hand firmly.

Morris went back to his partner and the two conferred.

"It's him. Positive identification from his passport. When we strip him down, we'll compare the tribal tat on his right shoulder. Glad his Australian whip boy told us he was coming to the country. Now, if we could get the two of them at the same time, Buddy, we'd have a fucking hot time down under, in, and all the points in between." Marcus grinned as he finished the sentence.

The two cops remounted their cycles and led the handsome Marcus to the Long Horn Diner.

The Diner was crowded, but Lana – part owner, waitress, and sometimes cook, always had a place for Hank and Mo. They were good customers, heavy tippers, and hey, it was always good to have two cops on premises.

The three were seated in a booth – Hank sat next to Marcus, sandwiching him in with no possibility of leaving before they baited the hook for the second time.

Mo made introductions as Hank and Marcus shook hands.

"So, Marcus, what brings you to our neck of the woods?"

"I'm here to discuss a work project."

"What line of work you in?" Hank asked innocently.

"I'm... in the... ah, entertainment field." Marcus answered, careful not to reveal too much – after all, they were cops.

The conversation continued with a review of the sightseeing Marcus had done in his brief time in the states.

"Hey, guys," Marcus stated as he gulped the last few bites of his chili, "I better haul ass – my appointment's at two."

He reached for his wallet, but Hank grabbed his wrist, "It's on us, bro." They shook hands and Marcus hastily departed.

The cops remained in place and fleshed out their plans for the capture.

"Damn, Mo, did you look at that ass..."

"I sure as hell did. I was examining the healthy package in front too."

Marcus concluded his meeting at five – signing a package deal of five porn flicks. Production would start in three days. He was already well established as a 'star'; and had quite a following of gay men, with over thirty titles on his 'acting' resume. He prided himself on giving the camera the best shots of his muscular ass and his twelve-inch cock.

As he drove away from the 'studio' – a converted warehouse – he rubbed his rod through the faded fabric of his blue jeans.

"Damn, wish I knew if those cops swing both ways – wouldn't mind doing a scene with them." Little did he know that the scene would soon be taking place.

Hank and Mo returned to HQ. As soon as Mo stepped into the building, he was told that the captain wanted to see him.

"We picked up that lowlife dealer today," the captain said as he referred to a stat sheet, "Street name – Tito."

"Good, Captain."

"When we put the thumbscrews on him, he told us a lot." Mo once again replied, "Good, Captain."

"He's yelling that he is gonna sue us for Police Brutality. Claims you and Hank kidnapped him and brutalized him after selling weed to you."

Mo remained calm, simply responding, "And...?"

"Just wanted to let you know in case the piece of shit pursues it. His word against yours. He's in lock up. Will be remanded to the county jail tomorrow awaiting trial. Probably will rant and rave all the way..."

Mo made a mental note to visit the county jail if he had a chance.

"Don't forget to write up your reports about the two purse snatchers and any progress you've made regarding their alleged kidnapping and brutality, Mo. Who'd believe it, Morris? Drugs have changed the face of the law enforcement world, huh?"

Morris and the captain talked at length about the newly-formed motorcycle corps. They had already apprehended one bank robber who thought he could escape the bank on foot. Traffic accident assists. Interceding in several street fights.

"Good enough," the captain concluded, "Good work, Mo. Now, go back out and get your next man."

"Oh, Sir, I intend to. Trust me."

Mo returned to his office. He conducted a search of registrations at area hotels. Success. Marcus apparently treated himself well – having registered at the five star West Diamond Lakes Inn.

He sighed inwardly as it was a gated establishment. A little more planning would be needed before the execution of the plan.

Before his interview, Marcus was confident that he would secure a lucrative contract. He had booked himself at the toney West Diamond Lakes Inn. Indoor and outdoor pools. Fitness center. Only the rich could afford it. Marcus was hoping to find a Sugar Daddy to treat him to the style to which he was accustomed.

He arrived and checked in, immediately calling for room service. He ordered a bottle of champagne and a steak and lobster dinner. Baked potato, lots of sour cream and butter. Raspberry chocolate layer cake. Even though he consumed heavy meals, Marcus never gained an ounce. He saw to that by exercising religiously.

He relaxed on the bed for a while before heading down to the fitness center. He worked every machine and felt energized after a good hour and a half workout. He showered, put on his ass and crotch-tight Speedos, and then headed to the indoor pool.

A sign indicated that the pool was closed at 5:30 pm. The lights were off.

"Damn!" he exclaimed as he tried the doors. They were unlocked. He stripped off his trunks and dove into the pool.

The pool was deliciously comfortable, just the right temperature. He swam a number of laps and then stretched out at poolside on a comfortable chaise lounge.

As he reviewed the day, he once again thought about the two beefy cops. He cock hardened as he envisioned what they would look like naked. Muscled, but just a little bit of a belly. Furry, like cop bears should be. He stroked his lengthening rod.

He played the scene with them in his mind. As he became more content, he dozed. It had been a long day of driving and he lapsed into a restful sleep.

"Fuck, bro, that was the easiest take down," Mo boasted.

"Yeah, who would have known? Our subject sleeping so peacefully…" Hank crowed.

The two cops, in full black Leather, had ridden Mo's Harley to the outside perimeter of the inn. Climbing the fence, the two had proceeded cautiously through a fire escape entrance and then to the subject's room up the emergency stairs.

Using a universal access key, the two slipped into Marcus' room unnoticed. But the boy was not there.

His clothes were discarded on the bed. A brochure with a listing of services was folded open and was thrown on the bed.

"Beauty shop... dry-cleaning... fitness center... indoor pool...outdoor pool," Hank read.

"Well, we can rule out Number #1..." cracked Mo, "although he is a beauty. My guess is the fitness center or the pool"

They confiscated the boy's carkeys and his discarded clothes and once again took the emergency stairs down to the fitness center and pool.

Only several people were utilizing the fitness center – a boy with golden brown hair was not among them, as the cops hastily exited to the pool area.

"It says it's closed, but let's take a look anyway...," suggested Hank as they found the doors to the pool unlocked.

And there they found their victim, snoring peacefully.

"Here's the tribal tat on his shoulder..." Morris remarked as he unzipped the Leather bag, which held their abduction equipment.

"Fuck, this is like taking candy from a baby, Mo," Hank whispered, as he placed a piece of duct tape over the boy's mouth. As a precaution, the cops had added heavy bondage rope around the boy's arms and legs. Gag in the boy's mouth. Hank retrieved the boy's discarded Speedos and hotel key.

If the guys were not participating in a kidnapping and torture scene, the picture would have been comical.

Two men in heavy black motorcycle Leather carrying a young naked man down the back steps of a posh hotel.

They were fortunate that they did not run into any guests or staff as they emerged into the back parking lot. They had spotted Marcus' silver Mercedes before entering the building. They quickly loaded him in the Mercedes and inserting the card in the gate, left the premises. The boy did not wake up during the capture. The two cops hoped he would not wake up until he was in their dungeon. Hank stopped the car, let Mo out to reclaim his cycle, and the two were soon home with a trussed up boy just ready for the cop's sadistic pleasures.

Hank pulled the car in the garage and the two men lifted the boy out of the backseat of the Mercedes.

They carried him into the dungeon and heaved him onto the work-over table.

Shackles were quickly placed around his wrists and ankles. A heavy Leather strap was placed across his waist. A heavy black Leather hood was laced into place over the boy's face. Only his nostrils and mouth were exposed.

The men joked as they placed the boy in bondage.

"Hell, bro, we didn't even have to strip his clothes off…"

"Nothing better than a naked, handsome porn star in your dungeon…"

Lord Aussie was there, ripe for the picking.

Marcus was aroused. He was no longer poolside. He attempted to lift his arms but they were restrained by heavy Leather straps. The same was true of his legs. His head was now encased in a Leather hood. Something was pressured against his tongue. He tried to move but he was held firmly in place. He struggled and attempting to yell, but it was useless.

As he attempted to regroup, he thought, "Fuck, this is a dream…"

It was then that he heard muffled voices near him. The Leather hood effectively limited his hearing.

The boy struggled in the tight bondage in which he was placed.

"Relax, son, we're big fans of your movies..."

The boy was doing his damnedest to speak, but the gag muffled his every word.

"Should I, bro?"

Mo shrugged at Hank's question as Hank pulled the gag out of the mouth hole of the hood...

"What the FUCK? Let me up... what the Fuck, are you crazy?"

"Relax boy... we just want to have a little fun with you..."

"Let me up from here, you fucking assholes. I'll have you arrested for kidnapping..."

"Well, Buddy, I know a cop you can call..." Hank taunted as he laughed at his own joke.

The boy looked unbelievably handsome, sweat covering his heaving body. His muscular chest and arms strained against the shackles.

"We gotta settle you down, boy." as Mo began massaging the boy's chest with his gloved hands. He reached down and pulled on the boy's handsome twelve inches of meat. Despite his fear, the boy's cock never retreated; it hung loosely until the massage began. It responded to Mo's excellent 'handling'.

The boy did settle down, "Oh, I get it. This is some sort of joke. You're from the studio, huh? A welcome party? What do you want, a blowjob? I'm good at that. Or, do you want to suck me off, so you can say you sucked off a porn star? Is that it?"

Mo was agitated by the boy's comments. He retrieved a heavy flogger with eighteen-inch tails. He stood back and lashed the boy's chest. The boy started screaming as the tails connected with his suntanned body.

He quickly began begging, "No, please, don't do that. I can't be messed up... I'm a porn actor; my body has to be in good shape..."

One of the men leaned down, his face obscured with a black Leather hood. He explained, "This ain't no fucking welcome party, you asshole. We're Leather sadists and we're gonna work you over. We've seen your pretty boy vanilla porn. You try to act like a dom – we're gonna give you some real-life experience. This is sadism, fucker. Now, relax, boy, I know how to control a flogger and I won't leave any permanent marks so you can trot your pretty ass in front of the camera when we release you." They placed a ballgag in his mouth to prevent further communication.

Hank retrieved a second flogger and the two cops worked the boy's chest and tits over like nothing he had experienced before. They played with his cock, squeezed his balls, pulling them down and inserting them in a Leather ball bag. Massive titclamps were placed on the boy's tits, which the two men then pulled on unmercifully.

Hank began rolling the boy's cock between his gloved hands and despite the boy's protests, his cock grew to its full twelve inches.

"Damn, bro, look at that piece of fucking meat," Hank said, as he pulled a box of clothespins off the supply shelf. Pretty soon, clothespins were attached to the cock's shaft. The boy continued moaning, protesting, crying.

Hank continued to pull on the titclamps and the ballbag between floggings.

Mo retrieved a pair of pinprick gloves and began slapping the boy's chest, his ribcage, his legs, his arms. The boy was covered in little red marks. His head rolled from side to side as the abuse continued.

Once they were satisfied that they had worked over the boy's front, they flipped him over to work on his back and ass. Hank roughly pulled the boy's cock down so that it lay underneath the ball bag.

And Session Two commenced. The two Leathermen couldn't wait to work over the ass. It really was handsome. Their Leathered hands squeezed and slapped the asscheeks until they were rosy red.

"Fuck, ain't that handsome, bro?" Mo commented as he pulled the flogger off his belt. The ass was soon crisscrossed with red marks to match the boy's chest. Hank flogged the boy's shoulders and upper back until the same pattern was seen.

The two men stood back to admire their handiwork. The boy was calmer or maybe the cops had worn him down.

"Well, boy, you won't be quiet for much longer... we're both gonna plow your ass with our manspades." The boy struggled, but somewhere along the line he realized that he would not escape the abuse until the abuse was over.

Hank crawled on top of the boy and began rubbing his Leathered body against the boy's naked skin. He played with his own cock until it was fully erect. Spitting on it, he eased his cock up the porn star's ass.

Despite the fact that his cock had been up many boy's asses, this felt great. Hank began moaning. Mo had retreated upstairs and brought back the partners' digital camera.

"May as well make a little porn flick of our own. Smile real pretty." Mo said as he positioned the camera to catch the assfucking. He then moved to the head of the table and spreading the boy's mouth open with his gloved hand, he removed the ballgag and inserted his own excited cock into the boy's mouth.

He warned the boy, "Don't you bite my dick, boy, or you'll leave here without an essential part..."

The boy dutifully sucked on the man's rod. "Actually, it tastes pretty good...," the boy thought to himself as he began vacuuming the shaft.

Mo thrust his cock further and further into the boy's mouth as Hank's cock rose further and further into the boy's rectum.

Both men knew how to prolong a pleasuring such as this, and the boy actually seemed to have calmed and was enjoying himself.

He began slurping on Morris' rod. His ass muscles began expanding and contracting to receive even more of Hank's cock.

"Good boy," Mo said, as he patted the boy's hooded head.

He eased the cock in and out, the tip of his cock stroking the roof of the boy's mouth. The boy continued to suck greedily.

Hank was riding the boy's ass, reaching down and slapping the boy's asscheeks, reaching down and pulling on the boy's cock. The boy's cock was throbbing. Precum appeared in the piss slit.

Hank began fucking the boy hard, ramming his cock as far as it would go. Morris began a more pronounced pumping as the scene came to its final climax.

Hank shot a load up the boy's ass while Morris released his cumjuices down the boy's throat.

The boy shot a load, squirting all over the workover table.

Hank dismounted the boy and crawled off the table and Morris withdrew his cock.

"Fuck, that was good, bro," Hank commented.

"Yep, but we better get him back..." The boy was lying calmly, heaving slightly.

As the two cops began releasing the restraints, the boy was attempting to communicate.

"Do you think I ought to?" Mo said to his partner, as he began to remove the gag from the boy's mouth. The ballgag was placed in the boy's mouth to prevent him from screaming on the return trip.

"He seems to have settled down... Sure, why not?" Hank said.

As the ballgag was removed, Marcus presented the cops with a big shit-eating grin.

"Thanks, mates. That was the best session I've had in months."

"Whaat?" Hank said.

"That felt so fucking good. What? Did you think my boyfriend wouldn't tell me about two hot cops who enjoy S&M?"

"But we kidnapped you...," Mo sputtered.

"Oh, I was asleep for the first few seconds when you picked me up... but when a big bear of a man throws me over his shoulder, I wake up... what makes you think I didn't know?"

"But your tirade here... that was pure outrage..."

"Mates, I'm an actor, remember?" The men escorted Marcus upstairs.

Marcus stayed for some time, sitting naked in the men's living room, absently playing with his handsome cock. All three enjoyed cigars before Marcus indicated that he'd better call it a night.

"I'll make sure you get my new videos, mates." He once again flashed his photogenic smile and headed back to the hotel.

CHAPTER 7

Taming Tito

"Officer Hernandez, I'm here to see prisoner Tito Fuentes."

The patrolman on duty apparently had not been briefed by Tito or his lawyer that Hernandez was, under no circumstances, to visit the prisoner. After all, Tito had been dragged off to jail claiming that Hernandez had subjected him to sexual abuse, had purchased weed from him, and was the co-defendant in Tito's lawsuit.

Hernandez breezed through the metal detector, even with a fully loaded gun, handcuffs, and other assorted paraphernalia that a cop ordinarily carried. The patrolman was just showing respect to a fellow officer.

Tito had actually caused some problems while in the holding cell and so, was now confined to a cell by himself.

As the door was unlocked, Tito turned from his bunk, his eyes widening in fear.

As he started to scream for the guard, Hernandez clamped a gloved hand over Tito's mouth.

"You'll shut the fuck up or I'll slit your fucking throat," Morris hissed, "you lowlife piece of shit."

Mo kneed the scared prisoner in the groin, causing him to fall roughly to the ground. A heavy, booted foot was soon positioned on Tito's throat. Gurgling sounds issued forth as the prisoner continued to struggle.

"Now, you and I are gonna talk... well, that is, I'm gonna talk and you're gonna listen, you worthless bag of shit. You've caused enough problems for me and we're gonna deal with it right now or you'll never see daylight again."

Hernandez roughly picked up Tito and slammed the boy against the wall, knocking the breath out of him and silencing him for the moment.

Hernandez now placed his knee in the boy's crotch area.

"What do you want?" Tito hissed at the cop.

"I said I'm gonna do the talking and you're going to do the listening, understood?"

"I ain't got nothing to say to you..." Tito began.

"That's right – in fact, I don't really give a rat's ass what you have to say, you miserable punk. All I know is that by the time I leave this cell, you're gonna be convinced that you don't have a lawsuit against me or you're going to be spitting up your own blood."

Beads of sweat appeared on Tito's forehead. "I got a case and you know it. You're a dirty cop. You stole my weed and then you tied me up and fucked me... you know you did..."

"And how many members of the jury are gonna believe your story, you lowlife asshole?" Mo said, as he smirked, "You've got a fucking rap sheet longer than your arm, boy. Not to mention warrants in Arizona and New Mexico. And, boy, show me your citizenship papers..."

Tito was sweating even more. "You can't fucking prove nothing. You're just bluffing."

"Am I?" as Mo reached in his breast pocket and pulled photocopies of papers that included Tito's outstanding warrants and evidence of an earlier deportation hearing.

"You son-of-a-bitch, that was years ago..." Tito cried as he lunged for the papers. Mo allowed them to be snatched out of his hand. Tito ripped them up into small pieces and discarded them on the floor.

"I've already filed the notarized originals with the appropriate authorities, asshole. It won't do you any good."

With that, Tito spit at the cop, a gob of it landing on Mo's cheek.

"I don't allow boys to do that to me," Mo said, as he slapped the boy across the cheek and pinned him against the wall.

Tito held his cheek for some time. Tears welled up in his eyes. "I don't want to go back..."

"All right, then. You cooperate with me and I'll get you a lighter sentence. You'll drop the charges immediately and tell your lawyer you were lying."

"How long will I be in if I do that?"

"Five years max... two if you behave yourself."

Tito shook his head slowly, finally saying, "Agreed."

"There, I thought we could come to some agreement." Mo said.

Mo lifted the boy up and slammed the boy's body against the wall, facing it. The boy did not resist.

Mo rubbed his cock through his twill patrol pants. His cock was hardening at the thought of fucking the boy one more time. He had always wanted to fuck a prisoner.

He quietly slipped handcuffs on the boy's hands and picking up a small towel from the washbasin jammed it in Tito's mouth, tying it behind the boy's head.

He quickly unzipped his pants and pulled out his hardening coprod. He pulled down Tito's sweat pants and underwear.

Without ceremony, he jammed his cock up the prisoner's ass and hastily pumped a load of jism up the boy's hole. The boy wrenched from side to side, but was impaled with Mo's cock until Mo had finished his business. Mo hastily wiped the boy's rectum and stuffed the towel in his pants pocket. The guards didn't need any evidence to support any future claims that Tito had been sodomized by a cop.

Quick and dirty – that's the way Mo liked it sometimes, especially when the subject was less than willing. He removed the handcuffs. Tito's ass was aching from the unexpected intrusion and his knees began to buckle. Mo threw him on the bunk where Tito lay heaving.

"That's a warning. You say any more and I'll fuck you even harder, boy."

Tito simply nodded as Mo repaired himself and banged on the cell's door.

Mo felt sure that Tito had learned his lesson and would cause no more trouble.

He hastily left the jail.

CHAPTER 8

Cop Vacation

It was vacation time for the two cops and they were packing their gear for a weeklong visit to Palm Springs and a meeting of the Fellows in Uniform Kink (known as F.U.K.). It was a meeting of men who enjoyed wearing uniforms and of course, practicing all their sadistic pleasures. Obviously, the men couldn't wear their real cop uniforms, but they had Leather gear closely mimicking their real-life profession.

With all their gear, they decided to rent a car even though they debated on taking the Harley.

"We've just got too much shit to take, Mo," Hank reasoned, "between the toys, and the uniforms, and boots; we've got a full trunk of stuff..."

"I suppose you're right," sighed Mo.

He enjoyed being on his cycle in full Leather gear.

The trip was uneventful and it took several days to reach their destination. They arrived at the headquarters, a swanky hotel reserved by the organization. A sea of men in uniforms with badges, Sam Browne belts, and spit-shined boots.

The guys threw their gear in the room and quickly joined the other men for a cigar party on the patio.

It was good to just cruise. More handsome men than you could possibly imagine. More than you could play with. Familiar faces, familiar beefy asses all covered in blue, black, tan uniform breeches, muscles rippling under tight uniform shirts, knee high boots, tight gloves, Muir caps pulled low over their handsome features.

Men's rugged features emerging from clouds of cigar smoke.

The two cops were in heaven.

"Damn, it's so hard to choose..." Mo commented as he puffed contentedly on his Churchill, "but I want to fuck another cop. I hope Sergeant Brinton makes it this year. Do you remember the session we had with him last year?"

"Not fucking likely to forget..." Hank smirked, as he recalled the non-stop fucking they had with him. "He is one hot fucker." John Brinton was six foot, two inches tall. Muscular. He had the deepest blue eyes, which seemed capable of piercing your skull. An easy smile that hid his inner horny thoughts of capture and rape. A pole that could impale a boy's ass. Black fur covering his body, even his ass. He was 100 percent top, but was versatile enough to enjoy the pleasures of two other tops. The three of them had fucked for hours. Full Leather. Then they had fucked buck-naked until dawn. And, last year at least, he was single. The two cops hoped that would be the case this year.

They scanned the crowd but did not see Brinton among them. He was a cop just like them and they had traded stories of conquest last year. They would have a few more to trade this year before exiting to one of their rooms for some man-to-man-to-man pleasures.

The cops continued to stoke their cigars and cruise the men.

A young Leatherboy, dressed in a black Leather uniform, approached them and softly said, "Excuse me, Sirs."

"Yes, son?" Mo replied.

"My Sir has asked me to invite you to join him for dinner in the dining room."

"Who is your Sir, boy?" Mo asked.

"Sergeant Brinton, Sir."

"Oh, very good. Tell him we will join him in a few minutes, as soon as we finish our cigars, son." Mo advised the boy.

"Yes, Sir. Thank you, Sir." The boy bowed his head and exited toward the door.

"So, Sergeant has a boy. Cute," Hank remarked as he attempted to undress the boy with his eyes. "Looks like he has a really sweet ass, just ripe for fucking."

"So we add a fourth to the mix. To do our bidding. I like how this week is shaping up already," Mo said as sadistic thoughts began forming in his head.

The men finished their cigars and trooped inside. They found Brinton seated at a table, his young pup kneeling beside him.

He rose when he saw Hank and Mo, and the three men greeted one another warmly. Slaps on the back, grabbing of the crotches, tongues exploring mouths.

The two Leather cops sat down and a waiter quickly appeared to take their drink orders.

"So, you've been keeping well. You now have a pup to look after you, John?" Hank inquired.

"Yes, he's a good boy," John answered as he caressed the boy's head.

As if anticipating their next question, he said, "And yes, you'll have a chance to play with him. You horny bastards." The men laughed easily as the waiter returned with drinks. Silence ensued for several minutes as the men selected entrees and sent the waiter on his way. The boy remained kneeling at his Master's feet.

"So tell us about your boy," Mo asked.

"He was one of my... 'clients'. And if I hadn't rescued him from the 'pound', so to speak, he would have gone to prison." John related that the boy was a J.D., in and out of trouble since he was eleven. He was convicted of armed robbery but because of his youth, he was sent to camp. He escaped. He added car theft to his list. "I'd arrested him so many times that he was given one last chance. In my division, we have a program where a cop can adopt a J.D. as one last opportunity to set him straight..."

"Straight, huh?" Hank remarked as his eyes viewed the docile boy.

"Well, yeah, little did the division know that I had other plans for this little fucker," John replied, as he arched his arm underneath the boy's jaw. The boy looked admiringly at his Sir but remained silent.

"I beat his ass the first night I took him home. He took it like a seasoned veteran. Come to find out, it wasn't all that different from his home life. By the way, his name is Johnny Boy."

The men continued to talk as their meals arrived and the conversation encompassed their mutual jobs as cops and some of the adventures and misadventures on the job.

Hank couldn't help but brag. "We worked over a porn star a few weeks ago..."

Brinton stopped in mid-bite, "What the fuck?"

Morris assured him it was true. "You've seen Lord Aussie?"

"You're joking? Right? That fucking hot ass and cock of his is enough to make any man drool," Brinton responded.

"Yep, we worked him over in our dungeon. Got the digital recording to prove it. Just happened to bring our camera. We'll show it to you later."

"So, now, you guys are porn stars, huh?"

They related the tale of capture, omitting Marcus' prior knowledge of the possibility of kidnap and abuse.

With the meal finished, John invited the two up to his room. "Bring your cigars and your toys."

"Well, you didn't have to ask us twice, fucker," Morris concluded as they left the restaurant and made a hasty retreat to their room.

They quickly made their way to Brinton's room. Brinton was seated in a chair. He had placed his executioner's hood over his handsome face and was holding his heaviest flogger in his right hand. His deep blue eyes shone brightly from underneath the Leather hood.

Johnny Boy knelt beside him. He was still in uniform, but that would soon change.

"Boy, you know the routine. Get undressed. These Sirs would like to work you over just like me."

The boy rose and quickly stripped off his Leather shirt. The boy was heavily muscled and covered with tattoos. Big heavy rings were in each of his nips.

The boy then removed his boots and shed his pants just as quickly. His ass was a beautiful sight to the three men. The boy was hung like a bull and had a P.A. ring in his cock's head.

John slapped the boy's ass several times as the boy attempted to put his boots back on. The boy finally succeeded. He stood expectantly, with his head lowered.

John put heavy Leather bondage cuffs on the boy's wrists and attached them with lengths of bondage rope to the drawer pulls of the bureau. John hooded the boy with a heavy Leather hood. His eyes were covered with a snap-on blindfold.

The boy's arms were now stretched the length of the bureau, facing the mirror, and his Master ordered him to stretch his legs, spreading them as far as he could.

The three cops viewed the handsome boy, focusing in on the opportunity it presented.

Each man selected a flogger – Morris stood to the left, John stood between the boy's legs, and Hank stood to the right.

A flogging rotation began with no mercy shown. The boy remained silent, accepting the slaps of Leather straps across his ass, shoulders and back. His Master had trained him well.

The floggings continued, with the cops getting more excited as each rotation took place. Their mutual cocks rose in their uniform pants. They viewed the floggings in the mirror above the bureau. It made them even hornier to see the boy's back being repeatedly lashed.

The boy's back soon exhibited a meshwork of red marks. The boy never flinched. The boy never cried out. He was proud to take the beatings of his Master and his two hot friends.

The Leather straps continued to bite into the boy's back and ass. A tail would occasionally curl around and strike his nipple or his balls or cock. Still, he took the sadistic abuse silently.

By the end of the session, the boy's back was bloody. All three men were sweating, cocks hardened by the pleasure they got from lashing the young man.

John removed the bondage rope, ordering the boy to stand up.

"Thank you, Sirs," the boy said, bowing his head to each.

John toweled the boy off and swiped peroxide on the boy's back. After drying him off, John ordered him to "Spread eagle on the bed. We're only beginning."

The boy crawled onto the king sized bed and spread-eagled himself.

The three men pulled out their single tails and began lashing the boy's chest. They were careful not to strike the balls and cock, but nips were fair game.

The single tails accomplished the same task in less time. Soon, the boy's chest was covered in lash marks.

John smiled with a sense of fatherly pride, "You're a good boy." The boy smiled too and said, "Thank you, Sirs."

After cleaning him up, the men wanted a break and so, sat in the available chairs.

"How about a smoke?" Hank offered, opening his cigar case and offering one to John and then to Mo.

The boy was hovering as his Master ordered him to clip the men's cigars and present a lighted match to each.

After doing so, the boy once again knelt by his Master.

As the men stoked their cigars, the boy acted as an ashtray, presenting his tongue for the receipt of the Leathermen's ashes.

All three men were rubbing their crotch areas and soon, their hard-throbbing cocks were 'taking the evening air.'

"You know what to do, boy."

The boy knelt in front of Morris. "May I taste your cock, Sir?"

Morris didn't answer, he simply pulled the boy's head toward his manrod.

The boy began a slow tonguing of the head, followed by a thorough swabbing of the shaft.

"This boy is well-trained, John, I gotta hand it to you," Mo said, moaning as his cock disappeared into the boy's mouth.

The boy was talented and soon had Morris shoot a big load of manjism down his throat.

The boy licked his lips and then presented himself to Hank.

Hank wasted no time as he pulled the boy's hooded face down on his swollen cock.

The tonguing and swabbing began. Hank was lost to the conversation as the boy continued to suck his bone.

He too shot a massive load of jism down the boy's throat.

"Damn, that felt great. Good boy," Hank said as he slapped the young pup's head.

"Thank you, Sir. It was my pleasure, Sir."

The boy then knelt in front of his Master and sucked on his Master's handsome cock. John was used to the service and continued the conversation while he was being pleasured.

"He is a good boy, isn't he?" John answered, as he pulled his boy's head closer to his cock and balls.

John prolonged his session for as long as he could, but he too added to the manjuices the boy swallowed.

During this session, the boy's cock had hardened. It always hardened when he sucked his LeatherMaster's cock. As John relaxed, he noticed a drop of precum in the boy's piss slit.

He swatted the boy and warned him, "Don't you cum boy. This is men's pleasure only." The boy grimaced as his cock released a spurt of cum.

"Bad boy!" John yelled. He jumped up and retrieved a butt paddle off the bureau and gave his boy ten hard whacks with it. The boy squeezed his eyes shut, trying not to cry. John stood over the boy as he cowered on the floor, "You have disobeyed me! You little fuck up!" He gave the boy ten more paddlings and relegated him to the area next to the bureau. "Don't you move from there."

"I'm sorry, Sir," the boy said, with his eyes lowered.

"See that it doesn't happen again, boy."

"Yes, Sir."

The three men resumed their conversation, absently playing with their spent cocks until they had returned to a hardened state, smoking their cigars.

John, who had already unbuttoned his tight uniform shirt, pulled it off, revealing his two handsome tits.

Hank couldn't resist. He reached over and tweaked them with his gloved hands.

"Oh, so you want to play with Daddy now?"

"You know we both want to, you horny fucker," Morris said.

The three men were soon on the bed, in various states of undress, rubbing, fondling, tweaking, and pulling. Hardened man cocks were being sucked. Asses were being explored with gloved fingers, tongues. Man on top of man. Tits pulled, balls squeezed, tongues in throats.

All three were overly excited at the masculine company and soon, Morris shot a load in John's mouth while John's cock explored Hank's ass until it exploded. Not to be left out, Hank towered over the two after they had finished and shot his load in both John and Morris' face. The three collapsed into the bed together.

CHAPTER 9

Playtime

Morris woke first as the sunlight peaked through the edges of the window. The room was heavily curtained and only a small amount of sunlight was visible.

As Morris attempted to stretch, he found himself, still in Leather, tightly trussed with his arms and legs bound together with heavy bondage rope.

"Hank, wake up!"

As Hank groggily answered him, Hank said, "What the fuck?" He too was tightly trussed with bondage rope.

"What is this, John's idea of a joke?" Morris replied.

The two struggled with the roping but it was useless. They both knew that John was an excellent bondage man.

"That fucker..." Hank concluded as he struggled some more.

Morris maneuvered himself around on the bed. Johnny Boy was kneeling by the bureau, just as he was the previous night.

"Boy, get over here. Take these ropes off of us."

The boy, with bowed head, said, "My Leather Master told me not to move, Sir, until he orders me to move."

Hank yelled, "Get your fucking ass over here, boy, or there will be more hell to pay..."

The boy remained silent.

The bound cops continued to struggle as the ropes cut into their wrists.

The men started sweating from the exertion.

Despite the predicament they were now in, the men's cocks began to harden.

"Oh, fuck, bro, I'm getting a hard-on from the scene we're in," Mo stated.

As their ears became accustomed to the sounds around them, they heard the shower running.

"That fucker... I'll get even with him, you know I will," Hank stated, as he pulled on the ropes one more time.

After a lapse of ten minutes or so, John made his appearance with a big grin on his face. He sauntered over to the bed, still dripping wet from the shower.

"Well, well, well," John taunted, "two pigs trussed up just the way I like them."

Morris reared his head only to view John's cock, fully tumescent and being rubbed by John's meaty hand. His balls were hanging loose and relaxed.

"Want to smell my crotch, boys?"

"Very funny, John, the joke is over. Let us up from here," Mo said calmly.

"Hell, no," John replied, "I've got two captured cops and I intend to have some fun..." John replied. John walked over to the bureau and retrieved the single tail bullwhip used on the boy the previous night.

He put on his executioner's hood and returned to the edge of the bed.

He rolled Hank over and loosened Hank's pants. Hank was bucking, attempting to kick John. With difficulty, Hank's pants were opened and his handsome, meaty ass was exposed.

"Crack!" sounded the single tail as it lashed one of Hank's asscheeks. "Crack" as it struck the other.

"You muthafucker," Hank yelped.

"So, you can dish it out, fucker, but you can't take a few harmless whacks of the single tail?" John said, as he continued to taunt Hank and whip his ass.

"Let's see how your partner does," John continued, as he loosened Morris' pants and laid the single tail across Morris' ass.

Morris knew how to play the game. He simply laid there as the tail hit his asscheeks.

"That's all you got, fucker? I like it... go to it, boy." John proceeded to give him ten more hard strikes, drawing blood on the fourth strike.

Morris simply continued the taunting, saying, "Stop playing with your pussy whip. Bring out your meanest fucker."

John was disturbed at the comments and laid the whip across Morris' asscheeks repeatedly until Morris' ass was crisscrossed with bloody streaks.

By this time, Hank had caught on to the little game that was now being played as he shouted, "Stop tickling us with your pussy whip, John boy. We're sadists, we can take it."

"Then why did you scream as the first lashes hit you, pussy?" John reacted.

"I just woke up," Hank remarked as John returned the whip to Hank's assflesh.

The taunting and the whipping continued. John's eyes were gleaming as he continued to lash the two cops. His manrod was rock hard, standing straight and proud.

Finally, he halted.

He slowly untied the ropes and the men rolled over on the bed, rubbing their wrists and resting their sore asses in the soft mattress of the bed.

John grinned. "You fuckers. Just wanted to say 'Good Morning' in one way that you could understand."

Morris crawled out of bed and stood beside John. The two men kissed. "You fucker. Good Morning," as he pulled John's head toward his.

Hank crawled out of bed and stood behind John. As John and Morris continued their morning exploration of each other's mouth, Hank grabbed John's wrists and bound them firmly with the bondage rope.

Morris, knowing that was accomplished, pushed John roughly to the bed. Hank bound John's ankles to the bedposts.

Soon, the order had been reversed and John was being lashed by a single tail from each of the Leathermen. Cocks hard, the two cops proceeded to lash John with the same ferocity they had just encountered.

The two men were heaving from the exertion, however, John was lying quietly.

"Had enough, muthafucker?" Morris asked John.

"Oh, did you start?" John asked innocently.

"You shithead," Morris replied as he cuffed John on the cheek. They untied the ropes and the three men wrestled in the bed, sucking and fucking one another until 11 am.

Playtime was over for the moment. It was time to cruise for fresh meat, suitable candidates for their sadistic pleasures.

CHAPTER 10

The Marquis' Playground

After enjoying the services of two naked boys until 3 am, the two cops tied the boys face-to-face and deposited them on the end of the bed. The boys would sleep like that, their cocks and nips pressed against one another's. Hank and Mo slept in their Leather unifoms, with full intent of waking the boys and subjecting them to a whipping. After several hours of sleep, Hank woke with a hard cock and whipping on his mind. He woke his partner and together, they woke the naked boys in a less-than-gentle manner. The boys were made to stand in the middle of the room while the two Leathermen circled them, catching each boy's ass with a heavy Leather flogger. Double the pleasure.

After accomplishing that, the Leathermen fell into a deep sleep and slept until noon. As Hank arose from bed, he noticed a slip of paper had been tucked under their hotel door. It was from Brinton reading, "Hey, you fuckers, tuck your little boy toys away and join me this afternoon. I have an invitation for the three of us to go the Marquis' Playground. Brin." Hank shook his partner excitedly, "Mo, wake up, wake up... we have an invitation to the Marquis' ". Although groggy, Mo replied, "Are you fucking kidding? How did we ever get that invitation?" He sat up in bed – the smell of Leather scenting his body. His cock was instantly aroused at the thought of hot, naked men at his disposal.

He propped his elbow on one of the naked boys, rubbing the boy's asscheeks before giving them a healthy smack with his gloved hand.

"Brinton. Damn, it was worth the session we went through yesterday..."

The Marquis was infamous, especially among members of F.U.K. He claimed to be a descendant of the illegitimate son of the Marquis de Sade and was just following through on his inherited traits to whip and flog and sodomize male subjects. Who the fuck cared if he was really who he said he was? He apparently had a private estate and during the F.U.K. conference would invite a select few to experience the joys of his stable of handsome, hung men.

Hank quickly telephoned Brinton's room and assured him that the two cops would enjoy going.

They were already Leathered up and so, they worked over the two boys that had spent the night in bondage until time to meet Brinton. It released some of their pent-up energy, but none of their cumjuices were spilled. By all accounts, every drop would be needed for the afternoon's activities.

The men packed their toys in their Leather bag and headed down into the lobby. Brinton was already waiting for them. "God," Hank thought, "he is so fucking sexy."

Black head-to-toe Leather. Executioner's hood. His deep blue eyes were twinkling. He also carried a small Leather bag.

As they exited to his car, Brinton remarked, "We probably don't need these – I understand he loans out his toys, but you have to sign them out lest you think you can take a souvenir." Brinton grinned as he continued, "Same with the boys – you can play with them, check them out so to speak, but they can't leave the property..."

The three men drove west of the city, enjoying the scenery and crawling into the hills of Beaumont along Route #10. The directions were extremely detailed and with Mo acting as navigator, they arrived at a gated closure. Brinton pressed the button near the gate and before too long, a voice answered, politely inquiring who was requesting entrance.

The gates opened and the three Leathermen entered the well-manicured estate of the Marquis.

And despite their worldliness, their jaws dropped as they drove up the driveway. It was carefully appointed with flowering trees, clustered in twos and threes. Young, naked men were restrained to the trees, chained between two trees with heavy leg irons and wrist restraints.

Despite his cool facade, Brinton exclaimed, "Holy Mother!"

Continuing up the driveway, there were naked men chained to the front porch support columns. Several were 'draped' over the second floor balcony, their asses skyward and their arms chained to the wrought iron porch railing. As Brinton parked the car, the men continued to spot young, handsome naked men chained to outdoor furniture, in doorways of outbuildings, and to trees dotting the property. One or two other uniformed Leathermen had already arrived and were walking around as if in a daze.

Brinton parked the car and the three Leathermen emerged. A young naked man, with a heavy iron collar around his neck, approached the men.

"Good afternoon, Sirs, I am Silas. I am one of the Marquis' slaves. He has asked me to escort you to his dungeon so that he might meet you before you pleasure yourselves."

The men followed the naked Silas inside the house and down a flight of steps. More naked men were suspended from chains in the dungeon. Most were hooded and already exhibited evidence of flogging. Some had buttplugs shoved up their asses. As the three continued to stare, a man in an executioner's hood rose from a throne-like chair. He wore buttery soft Leather codpants and bucket boots. His chest looked as if it was sculpted from marble, handsome. A beautifully braided cat-o-nine tails with a silver handle was attached to the waistband of the pants. He wore armbands richly accented with silver and tight Damascus gloves.

"Gentlemen, fellow Leathermen," as he nodded in their direction, smiling, "I am the Marquis de Sade, the fourth."

The men introduced themselves.

"A pleasure to have you here. I see that you have brought your floggers and whips, but I invite you to use my toys as well. My slave Derek will escort you to the toy room.

There is plenty of food and drink, choice cigars, tobacco for pipes, poppers, in the dining room. Help yourself. You can play with the candidates as much as you wish, both inside and out."

"Thank you for your great hospitality, Marquis," Morris said, as he was the first to recover his speaking ability, awe-stuck by the opportunities presented to him and his Leathermates.

With that the Marquis pulled the flogger off his waistband and lashed the boy standing nearest to him. He continued lashing the boy as the men's cockbulges rose in their pants.

The Marquis smiled a knowing smile, "Ah, true sadists. My own kind of men." He reached over and tweaked the stiffened rod in Hank's pants, who was standing nearest to him.

The three men couldn't help but notice the bulge in the Marquis' pants, which had risen considerably since he started the floggings on the naked boy.

It was then that a naked boy, also with an iron collar around his neck, appeared.

"Ah, here is Derek, he will escort you to the toy room, while I finish my rotation on this boy." He continued flogging the subject as the men were escorted to another room in the dungeon. They passed a room with five Leather slings, all occupied with naked men. Several rooms had St. Andrew's crosses, all with naked, handsome male flesh attached. The men could hardly walk – their dicks fully tumescent. They approached a room with hundreds of floggers, whips, canes, paddles, bullwhips, and dildos. Hoods, masks, mouthplugs, ballgags. Titclamps, spreaders, vices for crushing cock and balls. A young man sat silently with an open book. Each item in the Marquis' collection was numbered and would be signed out for use.

"Good afternoon, Sirs. I am Kyle, one of the Marquis' slaves. I will be registering any equipment you choose to use today."

The men were dumbfounded.

Finally, Brinton spoke, "I'd like to try one of the Marquis' bullwhips – I saw an ass outside that I'd like to try it out on. Can you make a recommendation?" Kyle rose and brought back a bullwhip braided of black and red Leather. It too had a silver handle with the Marquis' monogram on it.

"This, Sir. It is of the finest Leathers produced in Spain. You will find it has an excellent strike, almost certainly drawing blood by the fourth strike."

Brinton signed it out as the other two Leathermen continued to view the vast array of devices.

Hank settled on a butt paddle with sharpened spikes on it, while Morris couldn't resist a cat with thirty tails. Each had a delicious metal spike at the end.

"Excellent choices, Sirs," Kyle remarked as he recorded the registry number in his book. "Enjoy, Sir," Kyle said as he handed each man his instrument of pleasure.

A few more men were arriving and so, the three hastened upstairs and outside to choose their first victims.

Each naked man was more handsome than the last and the toughest decision was where, and with whom, to start. But soon the three did. Brinton marched across the front yard to a beefy boy standing between two trees. He unfurled the bullwhip and after a few practice strokes, laid it across the boy's back. The boy flinched, but did not cry out. He was hooded and plugged with a mouthplug. His handsome arm muscles flexed as Brinton continued to lash him across the back and on his ass. Brinton turned his attention to the muscular chest. Brinton's cock pulsed in his attached cod as he continued to lash the willing subject.

Meanwhile, Hank chose one of the muscle boys attached to one of the front columns, paddling the boy's asscheeks with the studded paddle. It left a dimpled pattern on the boy's asscheeks as he continued to paddle. He drew out his own flogger to flog the boy's shoulders and back. The boy was quickly reddened by Hank's efforts. Morris took out his aggressions on a boy restrained to a garden trellis, his hands suspended above him. The flogger made excellent contact with the boy's back and ass, wrapping around and catching the boy's chest and nipples.

After their initial subjects, the men wanted to try their skills on more of the bound subjects. The number seemed to be infinite. As more men from F.U.K. arrived, the delicious sound of floggings and paddling's could be heard, echoing across the estate of the Marquis.

The Marquis made several appearances, watching at a distance, complimenting the men on their techniques. Pulling his flogger off of his waistband to administer some lashings to unattended boys.

The three Leathermen exchanged their weapons of choice for other instruments of pleasure/pain.

"What a fucking orgy!" Mo thought.

And it continued. As the sun sank in the west, the floggings and whippings continued. It became a more erotic experience as the night settled in and the party continued.

Cigars were pulled out and lighted. The lighted ends were applied to tit and Prince Albert piercings. Forced smoke.

Fists were employed when a dildo wasn't 'at hand'. Cocks were employed just as often. Cumjuice spilled out of boys' mouths and asses. Cocks were slapped; balls were pulled and crushed with gloved hands. The Marquis was seen humping, in turn, the four boys who were stretched over the second floor balcony.

Morris and Hank compared notes. Both concluded that they would particularly enjoy thrusting their cocks up the Marquis' ass. It was handsome and well-sculpted just like his chest.

As they were comparing notes, the Marquis approached them. It was as if he was reading their thoughts. He leaned against a tree and unbuckled his pants. They fell down to reveal that handsome ass.

Morris went over and began rubbing the Marquis' ass while Hank reached around and rolled the Marquis' nipples between his gloved hands.

Morris spit on his mantool and roughly shoved it up the Marquis' ass. The Marquis obliged, bending over further and tonguing Hank's cod. Hank's cod was soon pulled off and his dick was in the Marquis' mouth. It did not take long before the cumjuices flowed out of both men's dicks.

"Thank you, gentlemen. I'm especially glad that you *came*," the Marquis stated with a smile, as he refastened his pants and went over to a nearby boy and began flogging him.

"Did that just happen, Mo?"

"Fuck yeah, I just fucked a Marquis. I'm adding it to my resume – porn star, Marquis. Who the fuck is next?"

The festivities lasted until dawn. The memories of the event would last much longer. Who the fuck cared if he wasn't a real Marquis or a descendant of the Marquis de Sade? He sure as hell knew how to throw a party.

CHAPTER 11

Sub Cub

After a week of playing out their S&M Adventures, it was too soon to return to home and work.

"Not a bad thing," Hank thought, as he pulled on his tight breeches and polished Dehners. He and Morris presented quite an impressive pair of motorcycle cops as they cycled through the streets of the city they patrolled. There were more than a few admiring looks from women and even more from men. The two, of course, were more interested in their male admirers, always on the prowl for handsome victims.

The captain started the morning with his usual meeting. At the end of assignments and concerns, the captain announced that the Police Department would be participating in the city's annual Fourth of July Parade.

"Mo, I want to show off the Motorcycle Corps. Show the city their gift."

Mo groaned inwardly, but told the captain of their willingness to participate. After the meeting concluded, Mo called a quick meeting of the Motorcycle Corps.

"Let's put our best effort out there, men. Polish your boots until you can see your faces in them. Uniforms pressed. Ties straight. And don't forget your gloves... Let's make the city proud of its newest Law Enforcement effort."

The guys nodded assent.

Morris held several practice sessions on the training field at HQ. Synchronized turns, crisp. Morris barked orders like a Marine drill sergeant – after all, he was used to ordering submissive boys around.

The Fourth of July began as a typical steamy, muggy day and only got worse as the minutes ticked away prior to the Parade. But the Motorcycle Corps looked fucking hot. Each cycle was emblazoned with the American Flag and the pennant of the Police Department.

As the phalanx of cops rode down the street, cheers erupted from the heavily-crowded streets. A number of the spectators waved flags.

Morris led the brigade, his chest swelling with pride. His men looked damned impressive. The cycles gleamed under the unrelenting sun. The uniforms pressed. Boots shined. Mirrored sunglasses. Helmets in place.

As Morris continued down the parade route, one young man caught his attention. The young man was snapping pictures of the Corps with more than a passing interest.

Morris noted that the young man wore Leather. Morris flashed a smile and waved and the boy snapped his picture. As the boy continued down the route following the Corps, Mo noted that the boy had on chaps, a colors vest with the Leather Pride flag emblazoned on the back, Dehner boots, and tight Damascus gloves. A black rim beard and a pronounced mustache that bushed out at the jaw line.

"What a cute cub...," Mo thought.

The young man continued to snap pictures furiously and followed the Corps all the way to the end of the parade route. At the end, refreshments had been arranged for the parade participants.

As the cycle men dismounted, the young cub approached Morris.

"Sir, I hope you don't mind me taking so many pictures."

"Don't mind at all, son... I'm Morris. What's your name?"

"jim, Sir."

Morris extended his gloved hand and squeezed the boy's hand tightly. The boy had a firm grip.

"Nice to meet you, son. Why so many pictures?"

"I edit a newsletter for men who, ah, well, appreciate boots and gloves."

"Well, son, glad to oblige. You want a group shot?"

"That would be fuck..., er... awesome, Sir."

Morris rounded up a friend that he spotted in the crowd and had the guys assemble with jim squarely in the middle. The boy's cock hardened in his faded jeans as the men surrounded him. Gloved hands on his shoulders.

After the pictures were taken, jim said, "That was awesome, Sir. Do you think you would be interested in answering a few questions... only if you have the time."

Morris smiled at the boy, "Be glad to, son. I consider this parade to be part of our community outreach, and an article is well-appreciated, just as long as you mention that the cycles came as a gift to the city..."

"You can count on that, Sir," the boy responded enthusiastically.

After dismissing the Corps, Morris led the boy to a nearby shade tree. The sun was unrelenting and the shade tree provided some relief. The boy must have been roasting in Leather, but Morris admired him for doing so. "The sacrifices we Leatherfolk make, just to proudly display our lifestyle," Morris thought to himself. He actually didn't mind it, he enjoyed the mix of sweat and Leather on a man, or boy's, body.

Hank, of course, followed the two and introduced himself. The cop's Leather Radar was sounding loudly in his head.

"Sirs, if I could ask you a few questions about being a motorcycle cop... er, policeman?" the boy asked quietly.

"Don't worry, son, we call ourselves cops all the times. We even call ourselves pigs at times," Hank said, as he cast a glance at his partner.

"Now, what are your questions, son?" Mo asked, as he lightly placed his arm around the boy's shoulder.

The boy's cock rose in his denims. It did not go unnoticed by the two horny cops.

The Leathercops answered the questions truthfully. The boy relaxed as the two men joked and kidded the handsome cub.

After he had completed the questions, Hank said, "Now, we want to ask you a couple of questions."

The boy nodded and looked at him with eyes twinkling. His heart was racing. He had already fallen hard for the two cops – damn, they were really nice guys.

They asked more general questions – where he lived, how old he was. He revealed that he was still living at home with his mother, a recent widow.

"Sorry to hear that, jim, how long ago did your dad die?"

"Oh, he wasn't my father, he was my stepfather. We never got along. He could never accept my attraction to... ah..." as the boy's voice dropped.

"Boots and gloves?" Hank answered for the boy.

"Yes, Sir."

"Not strange to us at all, son. We wear them with pride," Morris confidently answered as he held up his gloved hands.

The boy seemed fixated on the gloves. Sweat beaded up on his forehead. Tears began welling up in the boy's eyes.

Regaining control of his emotions, the boy answered, "Yes, Sir. Just because he disagreed with me, doesn't mean I ever stopped wearing them…" The boy slowly pulled out a pair of Damascus gloves and with the cops' encouragement, put them on."

"And keep wearing them, son, you look handsome in them," Hank concluded as he grabbed the boy around the shoulder and hugged him. He made certain that he pressed his crotch into the boy's crotch area.

The two cops ended the conversation with an invitation for the boy to join them for dinner. "We're gonna grill steaks and ribs. Why don't you join us?"

"Gladly, Sirs." Morris wrote down directions to their house. Embracing the boy warmly with bear hugs, the two cops knew what they were having for dessert – a nice, juicy Leathercub.

As the two cops mounted their patrol cycles, the boy stood, in awe, of the two men he had just interviewed. He rubbed the crotch of his faded jeans, which already had a moist spot.

Several hours later, the grill was fired up and Hank and Morris were in Leather jockstraps and boots. They knew the boy would be there soon and they had prepared the playroom for the night's activities. While at their conference, they had purchased new toys, including a sleepsack, and were anxious to try it out on a willing subject. They knew this boy would be more than willing.

"He's cute, isn't he?" Hank remarked as he set the table.

"Damn cute. Can't wait to strip him down and work him over." Morris replied.

"Well, we don't have long now. There's a car pulling into the driveway."

As jim climbed out of his car, Hank greeted him, "Hey, son, back here."

As the boy entered the gate, his jaw dropped. He didn't expect to see the men in Leather jocks.

Hank pulled the boy into the gated backyard and hugged the boy. "We're glad to have you here, son."

Morris came over and greeted the boy warmly as well. The boy wore the same outfit he had on during the parade.

"I... I didn't expect to see you in Leather, Sirs?" the boy said questioningly.

"Well, son, its one thing we didn't tell you in our interview, but we are just like you. We enjoy wearing Leather. Hope that agrees with you?" Hank said.

"Yes, Sir," the boy replied enthusiastically.

"In fact, if you'd feel more comfortable, you're welcome to strip down..." Hank said suggestively.

"Yes... Sir," the boy said somewhat reluctantly.

"Ah, come on, son. You're among your own kind." as Morris squeezed the boy's shoulder.

The boy began undressing.

"Why don't you put your chaps and boots back on and leave it at that?"

"Yes, Sir," the boy replied as he continued to undress, discarding his clothing on a nearby patio chair.

The boy had a cute, furry body. Nice ass. Strong legs. Muscled arms. And that devilishly handsome face.

"Much better, son," Hank said, as he patted the boy's ass, "Much better."

The boy grinned.

Morris presented the boy with a beer and then returned his attentions to the grill.

The meal was soon ready and the three held a lively conversation with the two cops doing most of the talking. They talked openly about their Leather lifestyle. Hank casually brought up their interests in S&M. The boy revealed that he had a Master who had released him about two years prior to the day at hand. His stepfather loudly complained each time the boy left for a weekend of service to his Master. The boy knew that his Master would physically discipline him harshly if he did not appear. He withstood his stepfather's abuse for the sake of pleasing his Master. His Master had trained him well, but after two years, he felt that he had trained the boy to the best of his abilities and had released him.

Changing the subject, the boy asked, "Are a lot of cops like you – I mean, into S&M and Leather?"

"Oh, there's a small contingent of us. Most of us have to remain discrete as you can imagine."

The two occasionally reached over to flick the boy's nip or grab his arm. At first, the boy flinched but as the conversation continued and the men complimented him, he visibly relaxed.

After dinner was through, the men offered the boy a cigar. He took it willingly.

During the smoke, the men began rubbing their mutual crotches. Their cocks were sensing impending activity and were communicating with the men's horny minds to get on with it!

Morris rose with his cigar half-smoked. "How about a tour of our house, son?"

"Oh, certainly, thank you, Sir. I'd enjoy that." As the two led the boy into the house, they pointed out some of the erotic artwork lining the walls. The boy was impressed, often exclaiming "Awesome." Several were photos by a well-known Leather photographer showing Hank and Morris engaged in sexual activities.

As the two men led the boy into the dungeon, he went willingly. "Awesome," was his only verbal response. The boy's cock twitched and was soon saluting the two men.

As Morris led the boy to the workover table, the boy lay down willingly. His wrists were manacled over his head. His booted feet were placed in restraints.

"We're going to hood you, son," as Morris presented the hood and slipped it over the boy's head. His twinkling green eyes showed acceptance and excitement.

The two men began massaging the boy's body. The boy's cock stood fully erect.

Putting on their tight Damascus gloves, the two men performed a Leather massage of the boy's body. The boy moaned. His head reared back. His cock was pulsing.

Hank began a light flogging on the boy's chest and upper arms and shoulders. Morris began a light flogging of the boy's cock and balls, grasping them with his gloved right hand.

The boy's head rolled from side to side, obviously enjoying the pleasuring at the hands of the cops.

Hank hooked his thumb in the boy's mouth and opened it wide, for the receipt of a puff of smoke from his cigar. The boy held it and released it as the well-trained boy he was.

Morris retrieved a heavier flogger and began a more intense flogging of the boy's genitals. He handed his partner another flogger, more intense, for the flogging of the boy's chest. The boy took it well. His cock never softened, remaining hard the whole time.

With his free hand, Hank began rolling the boy's nipples between thumb and forefinger. The boy's head rolled from side to side as the tit pressure increased.

After a substantial period of time, the men repositioned the boy so that his ass and back were now exposed. And the flogging, more intense, began. Slapping the asscheeks, flogging to create a striated pattern across the boy's back and shoulder blades. The cops' cocks were rising in their jockpouches.

"I can't resist that ass any longer," Mo said. He crawled on top of the boy, rubbing his loaded jock against the asscrack.

His hands massaged the boy's arms as he rubbed his crotch against the boy's beautiful ass. He fondled the neck of the boy with his mouth. No longer able to flog the boy's back, Hank marched around to the head of the table. He lifted the boy's hooded head and pulling down his jock, inserted his throbbing meat into the boy's mouth. The boy moaned but began sucking on the manrod.

The scene should have been captured on canvas – three males enjoying their masculine pleasures. Handsome bodies, accented with Leather, exploring, slowed down to a sensuous rubbing of male flesh against male flesh. Tumescent cocks, muscles rippling, sweat. Arms flexing, asses tightened by the thrusting of male organs. All three wished it would go on forever.

And it did for a long time. But the men could only hold their cumjuices for so long. Hank's cock shot first – a creamy load down the boy's throat. Morris came next with a mighty thrust as he gripped the boy's arms tightly.

Gasping for control of his own jism, the boy meekly asked, "Permission... to cum... Sirs, please?" With that he came before Morris and Hank could grant him permission. His cum slathered his fur-covered torso with a rich load of boy cum.

The two cops didn't punish him for this infraction. He would be ordered to hold it in the future.

The boy lay quietly on the table, the cum drying on his abdomen, while Morris and Hank discussed the boy's future quietly.

"Up, son, we want you to spend the night."

The boy got to his feet and looked at them expectantly.

They marched him upstairs to their large Master Bedroom. The newly-acquired sleepsack was still rolled up.

"Unroll this, son," Morris said as he pointed to the sleep sack.

Once unrolled, Mo simply pointed to it and the boy crawled in what would be his sleeping quarters for the night.

With his arms tightly by his sides, Morris and Hank laced the boy in.

"Look at that sight, Mo, snug as a bug in a rug," Hank remarked.

The boy had a satisfied grin on his face as the two men crawled into the bed they shared.

After the rigorous day, the boy fell quickly asleep, but Morris and Hank talked long into the night.

Hank woke first to find his handsome partner sound asleep. He reached over and stroked his partner's cock. Morris twitched and repositioned himself on his back. Hank readjusted his hand so that it now tugged on Morris' cock and balls. He eased himself on top of Morris who still was snoring peacefully. Hank pressed his lips against Morris' lips. His tongue parted Morris' teeth and thrust itself into the interior of Morris' mouth.

Morris wakened slowly, feeling his partner's tongue in his mouth. As Hank continued to massage his partner's mouth, Morris played possum. It felt good. But, with one swift motion, Morris rolled his partner over and was on top of him. His cock pressing into Hank's already throbbing member. The two naked bodies wrestled with one another. Their bodies in perfect alignment. Man nips pressed against man nips. It wasn't long before cum poured forth from each man's fuckhose. They fed each other their combined cum.

As they showered, the dialogue that had been abandoned as sleep took over was revived. The two let the boy stay in the sleepsack until the men had come to a decision.

CHAPTER 12

Born to Serve

The two cops trudged into the room where the cub was safely tucked away in the sleepsack. He had a peaceful look on his sleeping face.

Mo roughly kicked the boy, ordering him to "Wake Up!"

Momentarily disoriented, the boy woke with a sleepy smile on his face.

The two cops extricated the boy from the sack and ordered him to kneel before them.

Both were rubbing their cocks, full of morning piss.

"Drink from my tap, boy," Hank ordered as he thrust his cock into the boy's mouth. The boy gulped greedily as he tasted his man's piss. After he was finished, he automatically turned to Mo's cock and drank from that tap until it was dry.

The boy's cock was full as well. After escorting him to the bathroom, the two cops told him to join them downstairs in the kitchen.

The boy was ordered to make the men breakfast and after having done that, to kneel before them.

As the two men sipped on their hot, steaming coffee, Mo reached over to the kneeling boy's head and announced, "We have something we want to discuss with you, boy."

"Yes, Sir?" the boy responded as he looked at them questioningly.

"We had a long conversation last night about you, son, and we would like you to become our household boy."

The boy's eyes gleamed, shaking his head 'yes'.

"You would take care of our household and serve as our sexual slave," Hank quietly remarked.

The boy's eyes brimmed with tears, as he said, "I want nothing more."

"We will register you as a slave with the slave registry and you become our property. We will see to your basic needs. You will assign all your physical and mental ownership to us. Are we understood?"

"Yes, Sirs," the boy stated, as he bowed his head in submission.

"Come here, boy," as Mo kissed the boy tenderly. Hank reached over and did the same.

The two cops outlined what was expected of the boy on a daily basis and the boy readily agreed to all that they had outlined.

"Good boy." The cops finished their coffee and quickly readied themselves for a day of work. The boy was to return that afternoon with his possessions and begin a new life.

CHAPTER 13

Crystal Meth

The two men had quickly dressed and scooted in just as the captain was starting the meeting. A stranger sat in front of the room with the captain.

"Damn," thought Hank, "he's a fucking hunk." And he was, big and beefy, just the way Hank and Morris liked them.

"Men," the captain started, "we have a new member of the force, joining us from the Albuquerque P.D. As most of you know, Officer Banks is retiring after twenty-seven years of service. Hard to replace, but I think Officer Salzman will be a suitable replacement. Officer Hernandez, he will be joining the Motorcycle Corps."

Mo inwardly groaned. He was sorry to see Banks go. He was reliable and a solid member of the Corps, but Mo nodded and said "Welcome Aboard."

The captain went through the long list of assignments, reporting the possible emergence of a crystal meth operation in the southwest corner of the city. "I'd like to see Salzman work on this case as he's had experience with meth users in Albuquerque."

After the meeting concluded, Mo went up to meet the new officer. He was well-over six foot tall, with a black mustache, short cropped hair. He exuded an air of confidence.

The captain said, "Let's pair him with someone with some experience... let's put him with Foley."

Mo inwardly groaned once again, but had little choice but to obey the captain's orders. He motioned Hank to come forward. Hank had assumed that he and Mo would be heading out on their regular beat, instead he was told of the switch.

"Yes, Sir," Hank responded but it was a response without enthusiasm. He enjoyed working with his real-life partner.

The captain ushered Salzman and Hank into a private briefing room to tell them of the details of the supposed crystal meth operation.

Salzman interrupted the captain several times, to tell the captain how he would handle the situation. The captain was polite but was becoming increasingly irritated with the officer's lack of respect.

Salzman reared his chair back and began examining his fingernails as the captain continued to outline the information.

"Officer Salzman, this is a briefing and I expect you to pay attention."

"I'm listening, Captain, but I've been on at least twelve of these operations. A surprise visit is all you need. Surprise the faggots in mid-production."

Hank rankled at the use of the word 'faggots', but said nothing.

The captain reprimanded Salzman, "This is unique to us, and you will follow instructions as given to you. Understood, Salzman?"

"Yes, Captain," Salzman replied as he suppressed a yawn. He stretched his arms above his head and then cradled his head in them as the captain finished his briefing.

With the information, Salzman and Foley headed to the parking lot where the cycles were parked.

Hank inspected his cycle in preparation for their ride to the southwest corner. The day was to be spent gathering information from known informants.

"Foley, I got a plan..." Salzman started.

"Look Salzman, the captain gave us strict orders that we're to gather info today and that's what we're doing."

Salzman glared at him and mounted his cycle. "I say we ride out to the place and look it over from a distance. No harm in that. Get a jump on them. We tell the captain and he'll praise us for our actions..."

"That's in direct opposition to the captain's orders..."

"Look, pal, I've been on a dozen of these operations and I know what I'm doing..." as he turned the key in the ignition.

"You're an asshole, Salzman."

"I know what I'm doing. If the captain wants to sit on his queer ass and be a pussy about it and let these damned faggots rule the world, I say this man will take them down." He roared off the parking lot.

Foley was in a quandary. Should he follow or go back in and tell the captain of Salzman's direct disobedience. He chose the latter. The captain was furious when he was told. "I'll strip him of that uniform when I catch up to him." The captain put a call into Morris.

When Morris appeared in the captain's office, he was quickly briefed. "You and Foley go after him. Keep the damned fool out of trouble. Get him back here as soon as you can."

Morris and Hank mounted their cycles and sped off toward the southwest sector. The meth lab was located on a farm, apparently somewhere in the middle of a cornfield in an old trailer.

Both men were fuming. Retrieving this guy's sorry ass before he caused any more problems. They both wanted to throttle him for causing so much trouble on his first day.

It took the cops at least forty-five minutes to reach their destination, a rural setting, filled with endless fields of corn, soy, and wheat. Of course from the briefing with the captain, Hank had some idea of where the meth lab was located.

"He wouldn't try to handle it by himself, would he?" Mo shouted.

"He is so fucking self-assured, I know he will try," Hank replied, "He wants to be a hero."

"Well, the damned fool may have gotten in over his head this time. He doesn't know this area. Hell, I wonder if he even speaks Spanish?"

"Yes, he does," Hank said, "He told us that in the briefing. Among other things. He's a real homophobe, by the way. Referred to the gay blight that was affecting Albuquerque. Two cops on the force are gay. It's why he wanted to transfer."

"Well, partner, out of the frying pan into the fire," as Mo chuckled, the first attempt at levity, "And now two gay men are attempting to save his sorry ass. Ironic, huh?"

The two men rode for another hour and a half, crisscrossing back and forth across the farmland, before finally spotting a Motorcycle Corps cycle parked discretely at the edge of a cornfield. Salzman, of course, was nowhere in sight.

The two men dismounted. Their only alternative was to trudge through the fields. "I say we stay together," said Hank. The two cops parted cornstalks taller than either of them and were soon enveloped in the endless rows of corn.

Salzman had arrived at his destination and parked his cycle discretely by the side of the road. From past experience, he knew that meth labs were virtually undetectable if surrounded by vegetation. Still, there had to be a well-worn path to the location. All he had to do was to find it. He wasn't worried about the captain's reprimand. He'd bring these lowlife faggots to justice.

As he continued to walk and search, he reminisced about his days on the Albuquerque Police Force. It had been a good ten years. Well, eight if you count back to the day that those queer asses had arrived. He would never forget the day when Officer Pearce had announced that the Force was getting two cops from Los Angeles. Rosabello and Lilley. The cops were informed that the two men were gay. "Yeah," Salzman had quipped, "two fucking fair flowers from Fairyland." Some of the men hooted at Salzman's remark. Like Salzman, a number of men on the force were offended. And they made their feelings known. It was bad enough that they now allowed women on the force, but men who enjoyed each other's cocks up their asses? Fuck! The Police Force was supposed to be men, real men, not queers.

The cops were forced to attend sensitivity and diversity training sessions. Salzman refused to listen. He was a real man.

Sure, he'd been sucked off a few times by guys. Lowlifes who were hoping to have the charges against them reduced or even forgiven. That didn't make him a fucking queer. That just made him a man who liked to have his cock sucked. And when a gun was pointed at their head, most guys were happy to suck his nine-inch pole.

He continued trudging through the cornfields.

As he crested a small rise in the field, he spotted the glint of metal. As he looked at the object, some yards away, he realized it was a trailer.

"Bingo!" he exclaimed, as a pair of muscular arms pulled his arms tight behind him. He struggled, but another pair of muscular arms grabbed his legs. Ropes were tied tightly around his arms, chest, and upper legs. He had a chance to glimpse at two Hispanic men before a burlap bag went over his head. The gun muzzle never left his head as he was forced to walk rapidly toward what he could only assume was the trailer. He stumbled several times, but was caught before he fell. Despite his police cool, Salzman began sweating. He was a cop. He was the enemy. He had just discovered the meth lab and he had seen their faces. And he was on his own.

The two cops continued to trudge, occasionally spotting a torn leaf or a bootprint, which may or may not have been Salzman's.

"Damn his hide! Wasting my time on that prick...," Hank complained, "I say when we find him, we fuck his ass."

"We have to find him first," Mo replied.

The two continued their trek as the sun blistered down on them.

The two men hustled their captor across the remainder of the cornfield toward the shack in back of the trailer.

"Look, you take care of him... I gotta get this shit done and delivered before five o'clock or my ass will be grass," said Manuel.

"What am I supposed to do to him?" questioned Ray.

"We either leave him in there until we get the product done or we snuff him," Manuel said, with a growing agitation in his voice.

"Fuck, he's a cop, man. We'd get big time for snuffing a cop." Ray whined.

"You just gonna let him go, stupid? He's seen our faces, asshole!" Manuel replied.

"Well, then, you shoot him... You can even use his gun. Hey, maybe we can make it look like a suicide." Ray suggested.

"Now you're thinking, little brother. But first things first. Gotta get this shitload done. Put him in the shack and make sure he can't get out," Manuel ordered as he headed toward the trailer.

Salzman was being led to what he assumed was an outbuilding – the shack that one of the men alluded to. As Ray fumbled with the key for the padlock, Salzman realized that this was his only chance to escape. But with his legs and arms tightly bound, and a bag over his head, what could he do? He gave it his best shot, he bent over and attempted to head butt the unsuspecting captor in his back. Instead, Ray stepped aside and Salzman rammed his head into the door. The door was rotted and the force of Salzman's head actually caused the hasp of the doorlock to pull out of the rotted wood. Salzman fell with a thud onto the wooden floor of the shack.

Ray laughed, "Thanks, Shithead, saves me the trouble." With that Ray hauled off and kicked Salzman in the groin, the head, and the stomach area. Salzman doubled up in pain.

Using an old rubber belt from a farm apparatus, probably a tractor, Ray wrapped it around Salzman's calves, doubling them up so that Salzman's feet were now touching his asscheeks. He secured the rubber belting with several knots. A paper bag, discarded on the floor, was wadded up and shoved in Salzman's mouth.

Salzman was too weak to resist.

For good measure, Ray kicked Salzman once more in his groin, his head, and his stomach. He left the shack and marched toward the trailer.

CHAPTER 14

Rescue & Retrieval

Mo and Hank continued to trek through the endless rows of corn. Sweat poured off their foreheads as the sun beat mercilessly down on them.

They had been walking for a good half hour when they finally spotted what looked like a trail, through the rows of corn.

"Mo, here…," Hank remarked, as he pointed to footprints. They were old; the dirt was hard as a rock. These had been left when the ground was softer.

They followed the trail, which disappeared and reappeared.

"Here we go…," whispered Mo as they spotted the glimmer of tin in the sunlight. It was the roof of the trailer.

The two cops proceeded cautiously, circling around to what they thought was the back of the property. A trailer and an old shack were the two extant buildings.

"Let's check the shack first…" Mo suggested as they drew their guns. Hank eased his way to the back of the shack.

One grimy window, covered with vines including a healthy crop of poison ivy, appeared on the reverse side of the building. Hank eased himself up to the window. He pulled the vines aside with his gun. The window was dirty and revealed nothing inside. Hank moistened the back of his glove and wiped one of the panes clean. He peered in. Salzman was doubled up and laying on the floor. He appeared unconscious.

"Fuck, bro, he's in there... he's lying on the floor."

The two cops eased around the corner of the building. The door was ajar. With Mo on one side, Hank on the other, and with guns drawn, Hank kicked in the door. It swung on its hinges and collapsed on top of the prone figure of Salzman.

The two men hastened into the building and after a survey of the building to make sure no one else was in the building; Mo guarded the door while Hank bent down to Salzman.

He shook Salzman, saying "Salzman, Salzman, can you hear me?" He removed the paper bag from Salzman's mouth.

"Huh?" Salzman replied with a grimace on his face.

Hank plied him with questions, "How many are there, Salzman?" but Salzman was unresponsive. His eyes were closed and his face registered a great deal of pain.

Hank untied the rubber tubing that confined Salzman's legs. He gently stretched Salzman's legs out to full length.

"We gotta get him out of here... he needs medical attention," Mo said, as he noted a large bruised area on Salzman's forehead.

Mo called on his wireless. "Officer down. Officer down. We need medical back up and police back up...." He gave the location as best he could.

Using their training for medical emergencies, the two men lifted Salzman as gently as possible, one grabbing him under his arms and the other carrying his legs out of the building. If they were lucky, they could get him far enough away from the trailer before returning to apprehend the Crystal Meth proprietors.

The men hunkered down and walked as swiftly as possible. Salzman was lapsing in and out of consciousness as his aching body was jostled. Once or twice, he yelled loudly.

Despite his sympathy for the situation, Hank warned Salzman to "Shut the fuck up! We need to get you away from the situation as quickly as possible."

The cops had only traversed about fifty feet when they heard yelling behind them.

"Stop right there, you muthafuckers," and a blast of shots rang perilously close to them.

As gently as possible, they lowered Salzman and flopped down on their stomachs, drawing their guns.

The man stood near the trailer, aiming his rifle with closer precision. "I'll take you muthafuckers out one by one," he said, as he began to walk toward them, in a zigzagged pattern.

Hank positioned his index finger on his gun's trigger. Mo already had his gun trained on the man.

Another barrage of firing erupted from the man's rifle. The cartridges flew widely but were too close for comfort.

Hank and Mo both fired. One bullet apparently slammed into the man's right shoulder. He dropped the rifle and grasped the shoulder as blood began staining the man's white tee shirt.

"Let's get the fuck out of here...," Mo said, "we don't know how many more there are...."

They picked up Salzman once again, who was now breathing heavily. They had only marched about fifteen feet when they heard another man yelling at them. He came out of the trailer, witnessing his partner's injury. He picked up the rifle and shots once again rang out.

Just as they were deciding whether to take position once again or make a run for it, a series of loud pops sounded from inside the trailer.

They turned and saw the second man run back into the trailer.

"Our chance... let's keep moving...," Mo said, "I know what's coming...."

And with that, a loud explosion and the trailer was fully engulfed in flames. The Crystal Meth lab had claimed at least one victim.

The two cops debated whether they should go back and save the wounded man.

"Our first duty is to our fellow officer," Mo reasoned as they continued to carry him further and further away from the scene.

Mo once again called for backup, adding a call to the Fire Company. They would not need directions – the flames were shooting high into the sky and threatening the dry cornfields. The two cops only hoped that the Fire Department would get there in time before the fire was out of control.

As Mo and Hank continued to carry Salzman through the endless rows of corn, they finally spotted a road and a number of cruisers. An EMT unit hastily placed Salzman on a stretcher.

As they administered oxygen to him, they reviewed the bruises on his body. The kicks had been life-threatening – Salzman was bleeding internally. A helicopter was called and Salzman was life-flighted to the regional hospital for the best possible treatment.

The police later reported to Hank and Mo that upon returning to the Crystal Meth lab scene, it was apparent that Ray, with the wounded shoulder, had made an attempt to retrieve his buddy from the burning trailer. His body was covered with seventy percent burns and was not expected to live.

The day drew to a close. It was a grim reminder of the dangers that police and firemen encounter every day.

Mo and Hank returned to Headquarters – paper work had to be filled out. It was long after dark when they finally returned home.

Their boy anxiously greeted them. "Sirs, you made the six o'clock news. Are my two Sirs all right?" The boy waited for an answer, tears in his eyes.

"We're all right, son," Hank responded, as he wrapped his arm around the boy's neck, "Now be a good boy and pour each of us a shot of whiskey and clip cigars for us."

"Yes, Sir," the boy responded as he smiled at the two men.

The three settled in for the short remainder of the evening. Five thirty would come quickly and the job would have to be done all over again.

CHAPTER 15

Tattooed Bikers

It had been a grueling week. With the Crystal Meth lab destroyed and Salzman laid up for several weeks, Morris & Hank were once again riding together. The list of investigations into drug activity and other illegal activities was growing longer and longer.

The men collectively groaned as their assignments consumed more and more of their time. The captain read through the listing of cases each morning – too much for a small police department to handle, but the men were duty-bound to tackle as much as possible on behalf of the citizens of the community.

Morris looked absently out the window as the captain droned on and on.

"Tattoo parlor on South 43rd Street. Run by an ex-con, nickname BullNips. Possible male prostitution on premises. Anyone want to tackle the case?"

With no one volunteering, Morris raised his hand, "I'll take it on, Captain. I'll need a couple of days to prepare for the role. Can't have two clean-cut guys going in, they'll sniff us out as cops right away."

"Okay, Morris, you and Hank – take Thursday and Friday to do some investigating and the weekend to prepare for it and get on it on Monday."

For the next several days, the two let their stubble grow. By Monday, they looked like fucking mean bikers. At least they thought so. The two relished the transformation. Monday afternoon saw them suiting up in their Leathers and mounting Morris' Harley.

"Fuck, bro. I've always wanted a tattoo. Now, I can claim it as a police expense," Hank said as he grinned a mischievous smile.

The shop was reached within a short period of time and was easily identifiable. A bull with a bull's eye target around his right eye was the logo on the outside of the store.

The two men sauntered in. There were hundreds of tattoo designs displayed on the wall and in books on a table in the waiting area. A young man, in a black Leather harness and black Leather pants was behind the counter. His arms and torso were covered in vibrantly-colored tattoos. Nip rings pierced his nips.

He let the men wander around for a few minutes and then approached them.

"Sirs, may I help you?"

"Yes, my Buddy and I are interested in getting tattoos," Mo said.

"Do you have an idea of what you want?" the boy inquired.

"I want the Harley emblem spread across my back," Mo said, as he took off his jacket and with that, turned around and flexed his shoulder blades.

"No problem. Bull can do that for you."

"And I want an eagle attacking a snake over my left nip," Hank said, as he stripped off his jacket and pulled his tee shirt off as well.

"Bull can do that too… Let me write up a work order and an estimate."

As the boy worked on the estimate, the front door opened and a big muscular, black man walked in. His arm and pec muscles flexed as he marched across the waiting room.

"Can I help you?" as he eyed the two suspiciously. He looked them over, head to toe.

"Yep, we've come for tattoos. Heard you are one of the best in the area."

Bullnips' face remained impassive.

"That your bike out front?"

"Yes, it's mine," Mo answered coolly.

"Well, my boy will get back to you shortly. We require a fifty percent deposit before the work begins and the balance when the work is done. Think it over and let us know." Bull answered as he sauntered across the room and disappeared behind a closed door.

The phone rang at this point and the boy retreated to the counter to answer it.

"He's on to us," Hank whispered, "he's checking the cycle tag out as we speak. You know it."

"It's taken care of. Don't worry," Mo whispered conspiratorially, "I almost forgot to give you this driver's license."

He slipped it to Hank and whispered, "You're Tom Lazarus, ex-con."

"What?"

"I'm Allesandro Martinez, ex-con. Everything's cool. It gives us a kinship with Bull"

Hank slipped the fake identification into his wallet.

The boy once again approached them and handed them estimates. Hank's eagle would cost $350.00 and Morris' Harley wings would cost $650.00.

While the guys re-read the estimates, BullNips reappeared from behind the closed door.

He looked more relaxed as he approached them.

"Well, do we have a deal?" he simply asked.

"Yes, we do," Mo answered, as he pulled a wad of bills out of his pocket. "I'll pay the deposit for Tom. He can pay me back." With that he handed Bull $500.00.

Bull carefully recounted it. "I have both emblems in stock, but it will take some time to find them. Come back tomorrow. Around this time."

"Wait," Mo said. Bull spun around, looking angry.

"We need a receipt," Mo said. Bull's nostrils flared as he started to say something. He apparently thought better of it as he marched to the counter and ordered the boy to fill out a cash receipt.

He disappeared, once again, behind the closed door, with the money tightly gripped in his hand.

The men pretended an interest in the items in the display counter – tit rings with magnetic balls, jewels, and the like.

The boy looked nervously in the direction of the closed door and said in a low voice, "He doesn't like his authority questioned."

"How does he treat you?" Hank asked.

"Fine, Sir, just fine," the boy answered with his eyes lowered.

The two men said nothing more, but both had concluded differently.

Mo thanked him for the receipt and left the store. They remounted the cycle and headed home.

jim, their submissive pup, greeted them at the front door. As was expected of him, he wore his chaps, boots, and gloves. Each of the men gave him a healthy slap on the ass and commanded him to retrieve cigars and brandy.

The two men settled down in the den with their cigars and brandy. Their handsome pup knelt between them, serving as a willing ashtray as the ash lengthened on their respective cigars.

It turned out the boy was a decent cook and as a surprise, had fixed the men a healthy dinner. The men approved and nodded their approval to the boy as they consumed the meal he had prepared.

The boy knelt between them and they took time to rub his head and shoulders between bites.

As the boy cleaned up the dishes, the two men retreated once again to their half-smoked cigars.

They discussed the progress of the case and their game plan for the next day.

Once finished, the submissive knelt before them with bowed head.

Mo pulled him over and positioned him between his booted feet. He unbuckled his patrol pants and eased his cock out of his Leather jock.

"Pup want to taste Daddy's cock after its long day in its Leather jock?"

"Yes, Sir," the boy responded enthusiastically as he began to lick the head of Morris' cock.

Morris reared his head back and blew a ring of smoke toward the ceiling. The tonguing was relaxing and erotic. Morris pushed the boy's head down so that the boy was sucking on the entire shaft.

Hank sat quietly, fingering his own cock through his patrol pants. A substantial tent had formed in the crotch of Hank's pants.

After a long day of work, Morris needed very little time to shoot his cum down the boy's throat. The boy moaned as the cum coursed down his throat.

Once Morris was pleasured, the boy needed no coaxing into positioning himself between Hank's legs.

"May I, Sir?"

Hank nodded 'Yes' as the boy unzipped the pants and a Leather-covered pole greeted the boy.

The boy first moistened the Leather jock, flicking his tongue to the side where the cock's shaft was fully exposed. The boy's tongue flicked the entire pole with his spit before concentrating on Hank's balls, which were now hanging loosely outside the jock.

Hank had put on his tight Damascus gloves and was rubbing and pulling on his nips. It was increasing his sexual excitement as the cum began to rise in his manshaft.

The boy gently pulled the jock down below the cop's balls and began sucking the head of Hank's cock.

Hank rubbed his tits more vigorously. The cum was collecting in the shaft of his cock. The boy continued to suck on the cock's head and with every other stroke, enveloped the shaft in his mouth.

Hank stopped rubbing his nips momentarily to push the boy's head closer to the base of his swollen cock.

He pulled on his tits, his head reared back and with a mighty thrust, the cum came pouring out of his pisshole into the boy's thirsty mouth. The boy did not spill a drop as he moaned with pleasure.

"Good boy," Hank sighed, as he patted the pup's head.

"We're not through, yet, son." Morris quietly said, "Present your ass to us." The boy crawled around the floor until his ass was elevated and positioned between the two.

Pulling on his Damascus gloves, Morris greased the left glove with some lube, retrieved from the side table. First two fingers, then four, and finally the thumb began exploring the boy's tender fuckhole.

The boy moaned but said nothing.

Morris wiggled his fingers and finally the rest of his hand advanced up the boy's mineshaft. The boy began gyrating to the feeling of the fist up his rectum. Although he did not have much experience in fisting, he reacted very well. When Morris' fist retreated, Hank's fist took its place. It was a delicious feeling to have your fist up a Leatherboy's ass and both men repeated the process several times until they were both sporting hard dicks.

If the boy hadn't guessed the next procedure, the fists were soon replaced by his Sirs' hardened rods, one at a time. Mounting the boy's elevated ass. Fucked by a cop in full uniform, knee-high boots pressing against the boy's naked flesh. Pumping jism for the second time into the willing body of the boy.

With the night drawing to a close, the boy was placed in the sleepsack and the two cops headed off to bed.

CHAPTER 16

Inked Pigs

The two biker cops returned to the Tattoo Parlor as soon as it opened at 10 am.

There were two young men behind the corner, neither of which was the boy that was there the previous day. Both boys were similarly dressed in white 'wife beater' tees and worn denim jeans. They both had the 'lost boy' look, with deep circles under their eyes and emotionless eyes. Their arms were inked with various tattoos. They were whispering among themselves as the two men entered the store. The conversation stopped abruptly.

Mo sauntered over to the counter, "We're here to have tattoos done... we paid BullNips yesterday."

"Yes, Sir," the one young man replied, "but he isn't here... he had some business to take care of... Can you come back?"

"Why? How long is he gonna be?" Mo asked.

"I'm sorry, Sir, I can't tell you that..."

"Mind if we wait for a while?" Hank asked.

The boys looked nervously at one another, but had little choice as the two beefy bikers sat down and started absently thumbing through the books of decals.

BullNips yanked the door open and yelled, "You fuck ups! I oughta..." He stopped abruptly as he realized that the boys were attempting to give him a signal, motioning their heads and eyes toward the waiting area, that there were other people in the room.

BullNips did an about-face. He glowered at the two men thumbing through the tattoo books. Never apologizing or offering an explanation for his outburst, he stormed into the back room.

A frenzied whispering occurred between the two boys.

"Is there a problem?" Hank asked.

"He doesn't like surprises. He...," the one boy offered and then silenced himself as the back room door swung open.

Looking at Mo, BullNips said "Okay, let me start on your Harley wings... they're going to take several sessions, you understand. I'll do the basic outline and inking today. You'll have to come back for the shading."

Mo stood up and removed his Leather jacket and then his tight white tee shirt. He followed BullNips back to the cubicle and was ordered to lay on a table.

BullNips removed his shirt, revealing massive pecs and massive forearms.

"I need freedom when I'm inking," he explained.

"No problem, bro," Mo answered as his cock swelled against the textured top of the table Mo attempted to initiate conversation, but BullNips only grunted answers. He began to ink the contours of the spread eagle wings, the tips of which landed on each of Mo's shoulder blades.

"How long have you been in business, bro?" Mo asked.

"Ten years," BullNips answered succinctly.

"Where did you learn the trade?"

"From a friend."

The conversation lapsed as BullNips concentrated on his work.

Hank sidled over to the two young boys, who continued to whisper their conversations.

"Is this a good place to work?" he asked them.

"Yes, Sir." was the boy's brief reply.

"Do you get your tattoos free?" Hank asked as he grinned.

"We earn them, Sir..." the one boy responded. The other boy threw him a look, which conveyed, "Don't say any more..."

Hank was like a dog with a bone, however, and responded quickly, "And how do you earn them?"

"Ah, the longer we work for Bull, the more chances we have to earn a tattoo," the second boy replied.

"So, each month you work for Bull, you get another tattoo?"

"Yes, something like that," the second boy replied. He motioned for the first boy to help him with readying the second cubicle for Hank's inking.

As the boys exited the counter, Hank viewed two handsome asses in the faded jeans, which were provocatively ripped to reveal a little asscheek. As they maneuvered in and out of the cubicle, the jeans were worn in all the right places in the front too.

Hank followed them to the cubicle and watched as they laid out the necessary materials for his tattoo. The boys bent and stretched to retrieve materials from the cabinets within the cubicles. He was tempted to grab their asses, which strained against the light blue fabric of their jeans. He wanted to slam them against the cabinets and feel their cocks. Taste their mouths. Press his nips against theirs.

"How old are you boys?"

"Twenty-three... both of us." the second boy replied. The first boy cast his eyes away from the piercing eyes of Hank – Hank knew instinctively that the boy was no fucking twenty-three years of age. Of legal age, though – BullNips wasn't that stupid to involve minors in illegal prostitution. Or at least, Hank didn't think so. Hank let the conversation lapse for a few minutes, to let the boys think that he had finished his line of questioning.

He ambled back over to the books and began flipping through the tattoo books once again.

Mo's tattoo was progressing, but the tattoo was the only thing he had been able to get from BullNips. Mo's hard-on remained as hard as a rock as the big handsome fucker continued to work. His arms kneaded Mo's skin as he stretched it to tautness. The sting of the tattooing needle was actually pleasant to Mo. He wished that it was circling his nips or going up and down his cock. At that thought, his cock got even harder. Out of the corner of his eye, he could see BullNip's pecs flexing, the muscles in his arms bulging as the handsome man continued to ink the wing on his left shoulder blade.

"Always wanted to get a tattoo. In fact, there was a guy in the pen with me who did incredible work... Illinois State. Fucking guards confiscated his equipment time and time again, but he just kept manufacturing his own tools. I would have been proud to wear one of his tats."

BullNips did not respond, but it was obvious that he was taking it all in.

"Damn," Mo continued, "what was his name? The guys called him 'Striker'...."

A pause ensued, but finally BullNips replied, "'Striker' Russell."

"Yeah, that's it. Haven't thought about him for years. Wonder where he is?" Mo knew, he had done his homework, but wanted to see if BullNips would take the bait.

"Dead."

"How do you know?"

"His work was featured in a tats magazine. It said that he'd died while still incarcerated."

"Oh, shame. He was very talented."

BullNips neither agreed or disagreed, once again concentrating on the work at hand.

Hank rose from the 'waiting' area and returned to the counter where the boys were reviewing a tattoo magazine. The afternoon mail had arrived, but it was all carefully piled for BullNips to review.

Using Mo's fictitious name Allesandro, Hank stated, "Allesandro and I are gonna party tonight."

The boys did not respond.

"Yep, we got some premium weed last week – real good shit. You boys smoke weed?"

Both boys had looked up when Hank mentioned the stash of marijuana. It particularly caught Boy #2's attention.

"Of course, man," he replied, showing an interest in Hank for the first time.

"Well, why don't you boys come over after work? Share a joint," Hank proposed.

The boy was practically salivating at the invitation. "No," he replied, "that would have to be arranged through BullNips."

"What is he? Your fucking DenMother?" Hank said, irritated at the response.

The boy did not respond. Hank was frustrated – the longer he looked at Boy #2, the more he wanted to plow the boy's ass. He usually took what he wanted. Didn't need any fucking intermediary to arrange his man-to-boy sex. He returned to the waiting area.

Hank had no sooner sat down than the door slammed open. A big bruiser with tattoos and in heavy biker gear came storming into the store. He held the counter boy who had been in the shop the day before by the scruff of his neck. The boy's shirt was bloodstained and his right eye was noticeably blackened. His eyes were filled with tears.

"BULL!" the biker bellowed. As he marched through the shop, the young boys behind the counter drew closer together and lowered their eyes.

"BULL!!! God-damn it, where are you?"

Bull put down his needle and rushed out to the main part of the store.

"What the fuck? Can't you see I have customers...?" The biker looked at Hank, heaving from anger. Hank stared at him. The biker was about to say something to Hank when Bull drew him to the back area of the shop.

A spirited argument could be heard. Mo, still lying on the table, caught some of the conversation, the gist of which was that Ty, the counter boy who was now bloodied, had been picking up johns without Bull's knowledge. Pocketing extra money.

The biker, Bull's enforcer, had been made aware of the situation by another hustler, anxious to win the favor of Bull and become part of his stable of young men.

It was the biker who had roughed up Ty before he brought him to Bull for Bull's own brand of punishment.

"I gotta get back; I have customers... you fucking calm down. I'll handle it," Bull said to the biker. With that, Bull walked over to Ty and gut-punched the kid. The kid doubled over in pain. Bull kicked the boy in the ass and in the groin with his steel-toed shoes. He reached in the boy's jeans pocket and grabbed a wad of bills.

"By rights, this is mine, you little fucker," Bull snorted, "You got five minutes to get out of this store or I will rip your ass from one side to the other..."

Despite the pain the boy felt, he picked himself up and rushed past Mo, the counter boys, and Hank and left the store.

Hank jumped up, "What the fuck?"

Boy #2 said in a low voice, "Mister... Mister, don't get involved. Trust me."

Bull returned to the cubicle in which Mo was still stretched out on the table.

"What the hell's going on, bro?" Mo demanded.

"Just a little domestic squabble," Bull answered.

"What the fuck? That boy ran out of here bloodied and bruised...."

"It's been taken care of," Bull answered. Mo started to rise off the table, but Bull pushed him roughly back down. "I've got about ten more minutes of work, now stay still," Bull commanded. Mo was seething, but decided to follow through with the assignment.

Bull affixed a large patch to Mo's back, admonishing Mo not to get the work wet. "We'll work on the details tomorrow. You can get dressed."

Bull entered the waiting room where Hank was pacing back and forth. It had been over two hours of waiting.

"I'm gonna postpone your session until tomorrow. Something has come up and I need to take care of it." Before Hank could protest, Bull exited the store.

Hank approached the two boys at the counter, "What the fuck is going on?"

"Ty crossed the line and is paying for it," was the reply of Boy #1.

"What do you mean?"

The boy just shrugged and would say no more.

The two cops left, heading home for the day.

Once they had settled in for cigars, which had been clipped by boy jim, they compared notes. The case was cracking wide open, but they needed to talk to Ty to verify their suppositions. They hoped they could find him before he was brutalized any further. The boy had prepared dinner and the men sat down for the meal. They gulped it greedily.

"I say we head to Roosevelt Park again. Check out anyone who might know Ty."

CHAPTER 17

Ty's Confession

The two cops suited up in their cycle gear and headed toward Roosevelt Park aboard Mo's Harley.

The Park was crowded as the sun sunk slowly below the horizon. Clusters of young men were absently chatting and dragging on cigarettes.

Mo parked his cycle and the two men lighted cigars before entering the park. It was one of the public spaces where you could still smoke and smokers congregated to pollute the air with their smoke.

The men stood at a distance, surveying the crowd.

"Fuck, Mo, we could be playing with our boy tonight," Hank complained.

"Duty calls," Mo retorted, as he slapped his partner's Leathered ass. Hank wanted to grab his partner's jaw and stick his tongue down his throat, but knew that Mo was right. The boy was probably in danger of retribution by Bull. If Bull hadn't already gotten to him.

It was a hot and sultry night and most of the men in the park were in wife beaters and jeans.

"Mo, over there, near that fountain – doesn't that look like the two boys who were in the shop today."

"Yeah, it sure does." The two boys were clustered around someone who was seated on the edge of the fountain.

"Looks like Ty."

The men moved swiftly toward the boys.

"Hey, guys," Hank said as the startled boys looked up from what apparently was an intense conversation.

"Oh, hi," one of the boys said, clearly embarrassed to see the tattoo customers.

"Getting a little fresh air, huh?"

Mo got his first good look at Ty, whose face was now bruised around both eyes. The boy's body was hunched over, his elbows resting on his knees.

"Saw you in the shop today, son. It looks as if somebody roughed you up," Hank remarked.

"You got a cigarette I could bum, Mister?" Ty asked.

Hank answered, "Well, son, as I was explaining to your buddies here, my friend and I have some premium weed. You interested?"

"I could sure use it, man."

"This is a little too public, guys. Let's go over there near those trees."

The two men and the three boys walked over to the grove of trees. Hank pulled out his precious stash of weed and papers and rolled five joints.

As they lighted up, the second boy remarked, "You guys are all right. Thought you might be the fucking cops when you walked in."

"Why would you say that?" Mo asked.

"You don't look like Bull's usual clientele, that's all."

"How so, son?"

"You were polite, too clean cut even with your stubble. Most bikers that come in are there for... uh, other things. Bull's radar went up."

"Oh?" Hank responded innocently.

"Yeah, he did a check on your cycle tag."

"Really? What the fuck? Did he find out anything about us?"

"Well, if he did, he didn't tell us anything. He just said that if you asked too many questions to alert him..."

Mo didn't want the boy's unfinished sentence to go unfinished. "What do most bikers come in for – if not tattoos?" The joints were loosening the boy's tongues, just what Mo wanted to hear.

The boy just stared at Mo.

Mo stared him down. Finally, the boy replied, "They're looking for sex."

"With Bull?" Hank asked.

The boys snorted.

"Hell, no, with us."

"You guys hustlers?" Mo asked, already knowing the answer.

"We're in Bull's stable."

"Oh, that's cool," Hank said, as he fondled his crotch, "What do you boys get for a blow job?"

"We don't get anything. Bull gets the take. In return, he gives us a place to stay."

The joints were nearly consumed, but Hank and Mo wanted to keep the boys talking. Hank rolled a second joint for each boy. The men pulled out their half-smoked cigars and lighted those.

Ty, who had remained silent, finally spoke up, "That's why I got beaten up today. I went with Mike to an assignment. Only the guy that I was supposed to suck was a john I had met privately. He complained that Bull's price was double what I charged him last week. The shit hit the fan with that complaint,

Mike exploded and punched me. That's when he dragged me into the shop."

"And then Bull caught up with you later, huh?" Mo questioned.

"Sure as fuck did. He gut punched me so many times, I can hardly stand up. My whole fucking body is bruised. Kicked me in the balls. I looked at them a while ago, and they're swollen. Fuck, how am I supposed to trick now?"

"Listen, boy, you need medical attention," Hank said.

"Fuck, yeah. I need a lot of things, ain't gonna get 'em," the boy replied miserably.

Hank was becoming more and more agitated with the boy's revelation.

"You boys want the same thing to happen to you?"

The boys looked away, not responding to Hank's question.

At this point, Morris took charge, "I'm taking this boy to the hospital. I'll deal with Bull if he has any problem with it." A silent communication between the two cops indicated that Hank should stay with the boys until he returned, gathering as much information as they could. Before he left, however, he warned the boys that they were to say nothing about Ty's whereabouts. Having formed a bond with Ty, they swore that they would say nothing to Bull nor of the meeting in Roosevelt Park.

Morris escorted the boy to his Harley and was soon on his way to the emergency room of the hospital. The boy was in pain, clutching his balls as the cycle rushed toward their destination.

Hank and the two boys continued to chat. The joints had been smoked and the boys were feeling more playful since the issue with Ty had been taken care of.

"You're all right, dude," Boy #2 said.

Hank slapped the boy on the back, saying "So, are you, son."

He viewed the young hustler with interest.

"Bet you give a good blow job," he began.

The boy's mouth opened as if to respond, but instead the boy dropped to his knees.

With his teeth, he pulled down the zipper of Hank's Leather pants. Hank's cock was ready to escape and sprang forth.

Within seconds, the boy had Hank's cock in his mouth, juicing it up, lubricating it with spit. It was obvious that he was a novice at cock-sucking, but it still felt damned good. Hank held on to the boy's head as his cock inched further into the willing boy's mouth.

The boy reached into Hank's pants and pulled out Hank's balls. They were lubricated by the other boy's tongue, who had joined his fellow hustler by kneeling on the ground.

The cock swabbing was a good release after the pressures of the day. Hank puffed contentedly on his cigar while the boys serviced him.

CHAPTER 18

A Deal is Struck

By the end of the fourth session, Mo's tattoo was almost complete. Hank's sessions had been completed and he was very proud of his eagle tattoo. Since there was no reason for him to return, the cops felt that BullNips might become suspicious if the pair kept showing up together. Mo traveled alone. By the fourth session, BullNips had loosened up a little – was less guarded.

Mo traveled to the Tattoo Shop on Tuesday only to find two young men behind the counter. It was not the two hustlers that had given Hank an excellent blowjob. It was yet two more lost boys. Both were wearing rubber tee shirts and skin-tight, faded blue jeans. Both good looking, fresh, not hollow-eyed like the others.

Mo made his introduction to the young boys, immediately sensing that he wanted to get into their pants. The perfect entree into a conversation with BullNips.

Within a few minutes, he was led back to the room where he once again laid chest-down on the table. The tattoo was in rich shadings of orange and black, with just a touch of red, blue, and purple inks. It looked fucking hot. It certainly turned his partner on as they played in the shower, in bed, and on the patio.

BullNips was shirtless as he entered the cubicle.

"Hey, bro, how's it going today?" Mo questioned.

"Not bad. Not bad at all," BullNips answered in a more jovial mood than Mo had ever witnessed.

"You got two new boys at the counter...," Mo began.

"Yeah." was BullNips's reply as he soaped up his hands in the nearby sink.

"Don't know how you swing, bro, but I wouldn't mind having both of them sucking me off...," Mo cautiously said, to monitor BullNips's response.

"Um hmm, that could be arranged," BullNips said as he lowered his voice.

"Oh?" Mo said as innocently as he dared.

"For a price. They're in my stable now," BullNips replied. There it was – the clincher. Up until this time, BullNips had never expressed a single notion that might lead one to believe that the boys were for hire.

"How much?" Mo said, not wanting to lose the moment at hand.

"Four hundred for one, seven fifty for the two. Satisfaction guar-an-teed," BullNips countered, drawing out the last syllables.

"For one night? Seems kind of stiff, bro."

"My boys are quality. They are excellent cocksuckers. They will suck your bone dry."

"I'll have to think about it, bro. When would they be available?"

"Give me a time and a place and I'll have them there," BullNips said, as he continued to ink the last portions of the Harley wings.

"Can I pick them up here?"

"No!" bellowed BullNips. He reiterated, "Give me a time and a place and I'll have them there."

"Okay, bro, got to think about it first." Mo would set up a sting operation, but it had to involve BullNips and not a third party. "Mind if I look at them a little more closely when we're finished."

"We'll be done in about twenty minutes. You can look as much as you want. Just don't mishandle my merchandise," BullNips warned as he continued the final touches. Finally, he placed a large gauze patch over the tat and said, "We're done." With that, he disappeared into the backroom.

Mo sauntered out to the waiting room. The two boys were lounging seductively against the wall. You could see their cocks through the faded jeans.

Mo was aroused and leaned his hardening cock against the front of the counter. "Hey, boys. My tat's done. Just needs to cure now, like smokin' meat." His eyes were viewing the young man's crotch.

"Yes, Sir. Meat needs to cure – brings out the natural juices," the one boy playfully said.

"Guess my meat needs some curing then," as he reached down and rubbed his swollen cock.

"Well, I don't have a degree in culinary arts, but I did learn from BullNips all about bringing out the natural juices in meat," the other boy said.

"Is that a fact?" Mo said, as he continued to rub his crotch.

"Yep, working together as a team, we could cure that juiced-up meat," the first boy said.

"BullNips and I already discussed the terms – when are you boys available?"

"We have several appointments that BullNips has arranged, but... uh, Friday, would be good."

"I think I can arrange that. I'll let you know." With that, Mo exited the store. He had a lot of work to do to set up the sting.

And if it meant rescuing two young men from prostitution, it would be worth it. Of course, his horny cock was pressuring him to take the boys with him at the end of the day and have his way with them. That was a foregone conclusion.

Mo traveled home and exchanged his biker Leathers for his cop uniform. He enjoyed the tight breeches caressing his ass and outlining his manhood. His shirt fit trimly to his waist and accented his muscular pecs. His black boots were spitshined by jim.

As he looked in the mirror, he fondled his crotch and sighed, "Work to do." He mounted his cycle and headed to HQ.

Once there, he reported to the captain that the sting was in progress and strategized how to take down BullNips and close the operation. Mo would meet the two boys at a hotel and whoever accompanied them – it most assuredly would not be BullNips. He wasn't that stupid. The cops had Ty as a star witness. He had recovered from his injuries and was sequestered for the duration. The other two boys were willing to rat out BullNips as well, although it would be dangerous for them as they were still working at the Shop.

The cops would storm the room and Mo would be taken to lockup as a decoy. He couldn't be exposed as a cop at this point.

Mo returned to the Tattoo Parlor the next morning. Yet two more boys were in place behind the counter. They wore the uniform of tight jeans that Mo had become accustomed to seeing.

"Wouldn't mind working them over too," Mo thought as one of them knocked on the private office door.

"Sir, someone is here to see you."

BullNips appeared at the door, but this time greeted Mo with a smile. As Mo entered the private office, BullNips even gave him a slap on the back saying, "Allesandro, just couldn't resist my offer of fresh pussy... I knew you'd be back, fucker."

Mo pulled $700 from his jacket pocket and placed it in BullNips' hand. His massive fingers curled around it and it quickly disappeared into his chest pocket.

"I want the boys to come to a hotel room at the Sunrise Hotel on Dallas – you know it? Friday. About 4 o'clock." Mo said, without hesitation.

"Done deal, bro. Just get your manrod ready. I test all my boys on my cock and those two are good cocksuckers. You picked two of my best."

"For this kind of money, bro," Mo said, "I want my cock sucked off of me..."

BullNips hooted, "It'll have to be reattached, bro." A broad smile was on his face as he escorted Mo out of the Parlor.

Once Mo left, BullNips placed a call to Mike and told him the details.

Mo arrived at the hotel thirty minutes early. The cops had already been there and installed the surveillance equipment.

The two boys arrived promptly at four with their escort, the biker known as Mike. He recited a list of rules and regulations.

Mo gave him just enough back talk to convince Mike that he was a mean muthafucker too. "Hell," he thought, "if I was a john I'd tell him for that much money, I'd do whatever I want. And I just might, to make it more convincing." Mike left the room, but he hovered outside. He sensed that this guy was trouble. He placed a call to the Tattoo Parlor.

Despite his desire to have his cock sucked, Mo told the boys he wanted them to strip and wrestle with one another. The boys complied, shucking their clothes and climbing on the king-sized bed. Their naked cocks became more aroused as the boys sparred on the bed. Mo rubbed his crotch appreciatively.

Mo coached them to take each other down. "That's right, boys, kiss each other... explore each other's mouths. Stroke his cock. Yeah, that's it. Fondle his asscheeks. Oh, yeah, feel that naked boy flesh..."

Mo was fully aroused. Trying to suppress his desires to jump on the bed with them.

He stood beside the bed as the boys continued to fondle one another.

"Bet your man has a big cock?" Mo asked.

"Damn right," one of the boys answered, "I couldn't swallow the whole thing when I first started working for him."

"When was that?" Mo asked.

"Three months ago. Bull rescued me from living on the street."

"Really? Does he pay you well?"

The boy, momentarily distracted from the foreplay on the bed, said, "Hell, no, he pockets it."

"What?" Mo questioned in a surprised manner, "You don't get paid for your... uh, services."

"Hell, no, he gives us a place to live." This information corroborated what the other boys had told him.

"Well, how much do you boys earn for Bull?" Mo stroked his crotch area just to throw the boys off the scent if they thought he was asking too many questions.

"About a thousand a week," the boy replied. The other boy was more anxious to play and caught the boy in a half-nelson. Wrestling continued.

Mo playfully slapped the boy's ass nearest him to keep the action going.

"How many boys does Bull have?" Mo asked, thinking maybe the boy was getting tired of answering questions.

"I don't know, man, I guess maybe ten or twelve. They come and go. One crossed the road and has disappeared. We don't ask questions. Now, why don't you pull your cock out and we will give you a supreme cocksucking, worth every penny...." The boy advanced toward Mo and started to unzip Mo's pants.

Just then, the door burst open and Bull rushed toward Mo. "You muthafucker, you're a fucking cop. I'm gonna cut your balls off and stuff them down your throat." He lunged at Mo with a knife.

Two of Mo's fellow cops burst through the door at that moment and caught Bull's hand in mid-air. He was not easily subdued even with Mo's assistance.

The boys remained on the bed, naked, trembling from the scene at hand.

Bull was finally handcuffed and led away. Mike was already cuffed and fuming in a patrol car.

Mo closed the door. The boys looked stunned.

Mo simply said, "Now, where were we boys?" as he unzipped his pants and pulled out his throbbing cock.

CHAPTER 19

Revenge

The two men settled into a comfortable routine, both at work and at home. Their Leatherboy jim had grown into an essential part of the household and was proud of his Leathercop Dads. He greeted them at the end of the day with a smile on his irresistible face. As they retreated to the den, he always had freshly-clipped cigars and their favored brand of whiskey ready for them. jim had become quite a cook and always surprised them with tantalizing suppers.

One day, the cops arrived home to find the hallway festooned with balloons and streamers and jim wore a huge red bow tied around his cock and balls.

"What's the occasion, son?" Mo asked.

"Three years ago today, I became your boy, Daddy." jim answered, as tears welled up in his eyes.

"How could we forget that, son?" as Mo pulled the boy toward him and kissed him tenderly.

Hank approached the boy and said, "And actually we didn't, son." as he extracted a small gift from his jacket pocket.

Two weeks later, the cops arrived home. It had been a grueling day and the two men looked forward to their cigars, whiskey, and a delicious meal. Only jim did not greet them at the door.

"jim? jim?" Hank called as they entered the hallway. An eerie silence greeted them.

"Something's wrong...." Mo said, as he pulled his gun from the hip holster. The two men proceeded cautiously as they inventoried their own house.

"Basement door's open, Mo," Hank observed, as they cautiously made their way down the steps.

jim lay on the basement floor. His hands and feet were tightly bound. A pool of blood appeared underneath him, a darkened stain on the back of his pants indicated that he had been brutalized. The pants were pulled up, but unzipped and unbuckled. When the pants were lowered, a broken-off kitchen mallet, used for tenderizing meat, protruded from the boy's anus.

"jim? jim? Can you hear me?" Mo yelled as he dialed 9-1-1.

The boy did not respond, but in checking his pulse, he was still alive.

"I'll check the rest of the house," Hank called as he headed back up the basement steps.

It seemed an eternity before the ambulance arrived. Mo had succeeded in cutting through the bondage ropes. But the boy's wrists and ankles were bloody from the tightness of the ligatures. As the EMTS members lifted him onto the stretcher, Mo noticed bruises on the boy's arms. His right eye was blackened. Mo guessed correctly that the boy had broken ribs as well. After the EMTS crew had gathered needed information, they disappeared into the night, with the cops following closely behind.

As the two men sat in the waiting room, they were stymied. They spoke in low voices, drawing enough attention simply by still being in their uniforms. "Who would have done this?" Hank asked hypothetically, "No forced entry. The obvious items are intact – TV, cameras, your watch was laying on the bureau..."

"A vendetta against one of us," Mo advanced, "There are scores of punks out there that would like to see us twist and turn in the wind...."

Their conversation was interrupted by the appearance of Dr. Rushton, who was on call for the evening. The man looked weary as he approached them.

"Officers, are you here in an official capacity?"

"No, Sir," Mo replied, "jim is my adopted son. He lives with me."

"And so, you are not here in an official capacity." Dr. Rushton replied, viewing the uniforms.

"No, Officer Foley and I were returning from work and came upon the brutality when we entered my home."

"The young man is in serious condition," Dr. Rushton announced, as he sat in the chair next to Hank, "He has several organs, including his spleen, which have been badly bruised, I would suspect blunt blows from kicking. Internal bleeding. He lost a great deal of blood from his rectum – pieces of the wooden mallet splintered during its...uh, insertion, and have torn the lining of his rectum. I'm not an expert on ocular damage, but he may lose sight in his right eye as the result of the blows he took to the face. He is in sedation. We've made him as comfortable as possible if you would care to see him."

"Yes, we would," as both men stood up and were led to the bed in which jim reposed. He looked so small and damaged.

"I'll leave you for a few moments alone," Dr. Rushton remarked as he pulled the curtains around the three.

Mo leaned over and kissed jim on the right cheek as Hank kissed the other cheek.

Mo assured the boy that they would find the perpetrators, and exact revenge.

The two men left quietly, returning to Mo's house. They'd lost all appetite – showering and climbing into bed as soon as they returned home.

Hank awoke sometime later with a full load of piss. With no boy to take his piss, he crawled out of the cozy nest and headed to the bathroom. A strong smell of smoke wafted up from the downstairs. As he leaned over the hall railing, he witnessed a blaze of fire coming from the downstairs.

He rushed back into the bedroom, yelling, "Mo! Mo! The house in on fire…."

Mo roused quickly and the two men grabbing their pants, which were carefully laid on the chair next to the bureau, hastened to the back stairs. They proceeded cautiously down the steps. Smoke was filling the back hallway but the men managed to fight their way through the gathering deadly fumes and exited the house. Mo's cellphone was tucked in his pants pocket. For the second time that night, he dialed 9-1-1.

A second eternity passed as the men shivered in the cool, evening air until a firetruck arrived. The first floor living room area was ablaze with flames. The fire appeared, at first, to be contained to the back portion of the house. A portion of the flooring had collapsed, however, damaging a portion of the dungeon's equipment and the wall of toys so carefully assembled by the Leather cops.

The firemen were quick in their maneuvers and after a good half hour or forty-five minutes had the fire quelled. The Fire Chief approached the two men.

"You were lucky to catch the fire when you did, Sir. Another half hour and you probably wouldn't be standing here."

Mo thanked the Fire Chief and added, "Can you tell what started the blaze?" thinking that it must have been a faulty electrical outlet.

"I can't say for certain, Sir, but it looks as if it was deliberately set. Looks as if the furniture was doused in gasoline. A couch was the epicenter of the fire. A pile of cigar butts was placed close to it, and they appear to have been smoldering for some time. Apparently, one fell out of the ashtray and ignited the couch. I'll have to send in the arson investigator tomorrow, Sir."

The two men wearily gathered up some necessities and headed to a nearby hotel.

Neither could sleep.

"Who would do this?" Hank pondered over and over again.

"As I said," Mo responded, "we have put away so many lowlifes it could be any one of them. I'll check tomorrow to see who has recently been released…"

Mo reported for duty the next morning but Hank took a personal day to assess the damage at the house. With all the excitement of the previous night, he and Mo had not taken time to look for anything beyond obvious robbery 'targets' – cameras, televisions, et al.

As Hank methodically looked through the dungeon, however, he noted certain items missing. Several of their best floggers. Two Leather bondage hoods. Lengths of bondage rope. As he continued through the house, it was obvious that someone had attempted to extract materials from the men's computer. Hank became more agitated when he noted that all the CDs were missing – some with recorded S&M sessions. Hank began sweating – some of the CDs could ruin their careers. Whoever held them held a Sword of Damacles over the Leather cops' heads.

"I have got to call Mo."

CHAPTER 20

Dark Days

Mo arrived at HQ, only to be told that the captain was looking for him.

He sauntered into the captain's office. The captain avoided eye-contact as he asked Mo to sit down. That was not a good sign.

"Mo, you've been an exemplary officer. And I have never believed the bullshit that these lowlifes say about my officers. However, a package was delivered this morning to HQ which is damning toward you and Officer Foley."

Mo's mouth went dry as he viewed a familiar pile of CDs and photos on the desk of the captain.

"These are of you and Officer Foley shown in compromising situations. The scum who delivered these claim that you and Foley brutalized him and pointed to pictures, which would indicate that he is the victim in these photos. Do you deny it?"

Despite a strong urge to do so, Mo simply said, "No, I don't deny it."

"I'm going to have to have you surrender your badge, and gun until we investigate the incident fully. You and Officer Foley will be on administrative leave until the investigation is complete."

"Thank you, Captain," Mo simply said, as he surrendered those items and walked out the door.

He mounted his cycle and headed home.

Hank greeted him at the door and the two hugged.

"Captain is expecting you to appear within the hour to turn in your badge and gun."

"Shit," was all Hank said, as he exited the house to head to HQ.

Relieved of their duties, the cops visited their boy daily in the hospital. He still looked so small and damaged, but a brave smile always greeted the men as they bent down to kiss him. A specialist informed them that jim might never regain full sight in his eye. A drawback for a young man who showed so much promise with photography.

Mo stewed about the situation. It was because of him that a boy lay broken in the hospital, his photography career silenced. Not the only career in shambles. He and Hank enjoyed being cops. He and Hank enjoyed being Leathermen with S&M tendencies. As he thought about it, he became more enraged at the lowlife drugdealer who had ruined his career. He would find a way to get even. Mo formulated a plan. Despondent at first, Hank knew that his partner wouldn't take the situation submissively. Submissiveness was in his vocabulary, but it was not a word used to describe him.

Several nights later, the men suited up in their heaviest Leathers. A cadre of equipment was packed in the saddlebags of the cycle. This mission might take some time but it would be accomplished.

They cruised the alleys and talked to the drug addicts and potheads that populated them. They were more than willing to talk for an exchange of cash.

It was on the fourth night of cruising that they finally got a solid lead on Tito's whereabouts. For it had been Tito that had turned in the evidence. He had been released from prison as part of an early release. He had quickly returned to his old habits, however. Dealing out of a doorway once again. Selling weed. Petty theft. Bent on revenge for the dirty cops that had put him away. He'd get even. The sons-of-bitches didn't know what they were in for.

On the sixth night, the men set out once again with the stock of supplies in Hank's truck.

The men wore billed caps so that their features were disguised.

"Hey, man, got some premium weed for you," said the voice from a darkened doorway.

A meaty fist grabbed Tito around the throat, "That's not all you're gonna give me, fucker," as a second fist gut-punched him.

There was a look of terror in Tito's face as he recognized the hostile eyes of the two cops he had brought down.

"Want to have a little discussion with you, you muthafucker," one of the cops said, as Tito began choking.

"I...didn't mean..." Tito gurgled.

He was punched in the stomach repeatedly, "That's for roughing up our boy. And that's for trying to ruin our careers. We're gonna have a prolonged session with you. No videos or pics this time. Just man-to-man-to-bitchboy," Hank had retrieved the bondage rope and tightly tied Tito into a neat package. He was roughly thrown into the back of the truck and taken back to the remains of the dungeon at Mo's house.

He was tightly tied into place on the bondage table and left in the dark to think about his future (or lack thereof).

The investigation ground to a halt as Tito failed to appear at the hearing.

Mo and Hank appeared in uniform, but without their badges.

They were questioned at length about their private practices involving S&M. They were never questioned about Tito's disappearance. If they had been, they would have had to have told the truth – after all, they were under oath. Tito was sequestered in their dungeon.

After several days, without the star witness, the captain could not proceed with the investigation. He had no choice but to dismiss the charges against the officers.

They were admonished for conduct unbecoming to an officer. Mo was relieved of his duties as the head of the motorcycle corps and in a gut-wrenching decision; Salzman was promoted to the head of the cycle corps. Mo and Hank would ride under him as their superior. It was a hard pill to swallow, but at least they had not been stripped of their profession. Their personal CDs and photographs were not returned, although it was marked as evidence and stored in HQ's basement – should the star witness every resurface.

CHAPTER 21

A Second Deal is Struck

With evidence from the boys, the charges against Bull were enough to convict him of operating a prostitution ring.

Three months after he was incarcerated, he was called to the Visitors' Center. He was told that he had a visitor.

His eyes raged when he saw the visitor, "What the FUCK are you doing here?"

"To see how you were doing, bro," the visitor said in a calm voice.

"How do you think I'm doing, you fucking pig?" Bull growled as he recognized Allesandro, or whatever the hell his real name was.

"Just want to talk to you."

"I ain't got nothing to say to you..." Bull said, as he glowered with contempt.

"I understand, bro, but I have something to discuss with you."

By the end of the conversation, Bull had settled down and was listening intently to all that Mo had to say.

"I'll be back in three or four days. You think about it," Mo said, as he stood up and left.

Bull had plenty to think about back in his cell.

When Bull was told he had a visitor four days later, he smiled a broad grin as he entered the reception area.

"Well?"

"You got a deal, bro," as Bull pressed the palm of his hand against the plexiglas, which separated the two.

Mo pressed his hand against the plexi in agreement.

"See you in a few years, bro."

Five years, three months later, Bull was released. He had not forgotten the deal and as a free man, headed to a new destination.

Two Leatherclad men greeted him at the destination and they greeted one another warmly.

"Want to see your new establishment?"

"Anxious to see it, bro," Bull said.

The place was handsomely furnished. The first floor was a tattoo parlor. The second floor was outfitted with several bedrooms for vanilla pleasures. The basement was outfitted for S&M pleasures.

Mo, Hank, and Bull had entered into partnership. A male brothel run by an ex-con and two cops.

"We want you to meet our fourth partner."

"What the fuck – you didn't say nothing about a fourth partner..." Bull sputtered as he became visibly agitated.

"Relax... he's not really a partner, just a willing participant."

With that they escorted a slender Hispanic from a back room. He was hooded with a plug in his mouth.

"This is Tito... he's the first boy in our stable. If men have a taste for whipping or S&M pleasuring, he will be our prime whipping boy. Won't you, boy?"

Tito merely shook his head and sank to his knees as he began rubbing his plugged mouth against Bull's crotch.

"He's a very willing boy."

It was less than twenty-four hours later when the first customer arrived.

A devilishly handsome man appeared at the reception area. He was dressed in head-to-toe Leather. A Leather eyepatch covered one eye. He carried a small Leather toy bag, assumedly with the tools of his pleasuring within.

"How may I assist you, Sir?" Ty asked. Ty was serving as BullNips' assistant after he accepted a formal apology from his former (now present) boss.

"Yes, I understand that you have accommodations for a man who enjoys administering pain."

"Why, yes, Sir, we do..."

After registering, the man was quickly led downstairs to the flogging wall. As he pulled his toys from the Leather bag, the whipping boy was brought into the dungeon.

"Sir?" Ty asked, "facing the wall or back to the wall?"

The Leatherman simply answered "Wall" as he continued to arrange his collection of floggers and whips.

"Sir?" Ty asked, "hooded? Mouth plugged?"

"Yes, to both... but leave the blindfold off."

"Yes, Sir, as you wish...," Ty said, as he left the two to the pleasure/pain session that was about to transpire.

The Leatherman picked up his first flogger and began lashing the trussed-up boy. The boy did not react to the first several rotations.

The Leatherman picked up a second flogger – lashing the boy with a little more intensity. The boy began to flinch.

The Leatherman took his favorite – a singletail with a silver handle – out of a special case – and laid it across the boy's back with all his might. The boy yelped and twisted and turned. He continued until he had lashed the boy's back to a crisscrossing of bloody tracks.

The Leatherman then pulled out a wooden toy and held it close enough to the boy's eyes for the boy to see the object. The boy's knees buckled and he pitched forward against the wall. He started screaming, but of course, the mouthplug in his mouth prevented speech.

"Why, what's wrong, boy?" the Leatherman taunted as he removed the plug. He wanted to hear the fucker scream.

"No, please, Sir... no, no...Aahhhh!" as the meat tenderizer was slid up Tito's rectum.

The Leathercops' Leatherboy jim was just returning the favor.

His two Daddies, in full Leather uniform, were witnesses to their boy's first flogging session. It would be the first of many until jim had exacted revenge to his satisfaction.

The two cops beamed, "He's such a good boy," Mo concluded.

Be aware – the sadistic Leather cops are still on the prowl for willing, and unwilling, subjects for their pleasure.

ABOUT THE AUTHOR

G.W. Leatherman Parks has been a Leatherman for over thirty years. He is a proud member of the Leather Archives and Museum in Chicago and writes frequently for FLAGSHIP, the newsletter of Fits Like a Glove. He has also been published in *Drummer and Cuir: For LeatherMen by LeatherMen*. He is a collector of vintage Leather, Leather artwork and photography.

This is G.W. Leatherman Parks' fifth book. His first book *Leatherdaddy*, second book *Leather Nazis*, third book *A Harvest of G.O.L.D.: Leather Bikers on the Prowl*, and *Packed Cod, Hard Rod* are available from Amazon.com, TheNazcaPlainsCorp.com or your local bookstore.

A HARVEST OF G.O.L.D.
LEATHER BIKERS ON THE PROWL

G.W. LEATHERMAN PARKS

Leather Nazis

Erotic Literature by
the Black Leather Gloved Hands of
G.W. Leatherman Parks

LEATHERDADDY
Erotic Literature by the Black Leather Gloved Hands of
G.W. LEATHERMAN PARKS

EROTIC LITERATURE BY THE BLACK LEATHER GLOVED HANDS OF
G.W. LEATHERMAN PARKS

PACKED
COD,
HARD
ROD